<u>The Chai House</u>
By: Priti Srivastava

Table of Contents

This book is dedicated to everyone who has ever dared to speak, knowing that their voice would shake or that they would be the first to say it. When you are made to feel small, it's scary to make others uncomfortable. Thank you for being bold.

PART ONE

Chapter One

It's dim in here. I won't complain because I can stand. I can even turn around. Not enough space for jumping jacks but I can do sit ups. I have water. And a toilet. It's absolutely the little things. I didn't expect much, why would I?

I was allowed to bring one bag. A suitcase would have been conspicuous. Even if I sometimes work at the motel. Maybe even more so because why would I leave the motel with a suitcase? So, I took my backpack. They didn't check it. Amma watched though. Supervised how she does. Telling me what to do, how and what to pack, instructing me is her way of helping. I understand why she doesn't trust me to take care of myself. Even though we never talk about period stuff she made sure to go through my shelf in the bathroom closet to point out my menstrual cup. Obviously, she refused to hand it to me. I wouldn't have thought to bring that. I was out of my head, or too into it. You know how that is.

Strange though, because Amma would rather die than talk to me about getting my period. I was so jealous of friends with moms who celebrated somehow, brought them flowers, took them out to eat, made them a special meal, showed them they were special. That this blood was normal and their daughters were important. Even if it was embarrassing for my friends, they showed they cared. But look how things have turned out, Amma is much more helpful now then their moms are, I'm sure of it.

She also suggested a few extra pens and handed me multi-tools. I didn't even know that she owned them. She insisted, "just in case". Did she take them from Raj or is it that she found them and hadn't wanted to throw them out? She loves regifting and hates waste.

So, I've got you. This, Amma didn't see. I snuck it in after bed. If she could read my journal she absolutely would. Now's the time to try this. I've been saving this notebook for a special occasion and well, this is one. It's a good idea to keep track of days and when it's not dim it is dark, so I have my flashlight and spare batteries for it and my Gamer Girl.

Today is a day I am grateful I'm not allowed to use devices anymore. Location services and all, they'd know how to find me.

I didn't tell Amma that I packed my Gamer Girl. I figured she would get stressed seeing that I packed it, start a fight and accuse me of making a mistake. I wanted us to have a peaceful last night together. I don't know when I will see her again. I thought she'd stay and share a story, but she was so transactional. Doing what needs to be done.

My Gamer Girl is so old there isn't any location tracking but I can play Snake or that rip off of Tetris when I get really bored. Which I am sure will happen. Amma wouldn't have wanted me to pack it, she wouldn't trust me to keep the volume down, not use it while the worker-wives were working. I could leave a text file on my Gamer Girl if anything suspicious happens while I am in here. I am not sure what it could say though.

'I am Swati, I had a good life until the fascists came and nobody stopped them. Including me. If you are reading this, I am probably dead.'

I can't say what my reaction would be if I found an ancient piece of video game technology with that journal entry. If I was the daughter of a Knight who found it, I'd have to show it to my parents who would absolutely, immediately, toss it into a fire. I won't write that entry until I absolutely have to. I have to have faith nobody is going to find my Gamer Girl. I am going to get there safely. So I can give it to Abha.

I'm back. I had to lay down for a bit. Another thing to be grateful for - I have a mattress, on a frame. I don't have to sleep directly on the floor. Padmini promised Amma I'd be safe by myself. But I am worried about my next travels. I may be stuck in a space with multiple people, possibly even men. Men who are running away. Who have not seen a woman in ages. And even so, how many men have been forced to convert against their will? I could be stuck with them, knowing what they've done. More women have been converted against their will, I think.

There is so much trust and I don't have any trust in these people to help me or Amma. Why would they?

I got too emotional earlier, thinking about what to write for someone to find. I can't stand the thought of nobody knowing that I tried. I may not have fought very hard but I am against the Knights. I stood up to them when I could. Maybe not at first. Or directly. I just didn't think I had the power to do so. I am just someone who helps others do what they need to get done. I've never had a job that required an interview. I've never had a paycheck. Who the hell am I to change anything? I am guessing no one even noticed when I was gone, I don't have anyone to notice I am gone. Well, maybe Abha.

Amma was so proud when she learned I was applying to medical school. It took a long time. I wasn't a dutiful daughter or a great student. I brought a lot of shame to our family. I got pregnant "by a boy". I was young and he was old enough to know better. Not really a boy I suppose. He was American. Mark. He didn't get into trouble. I did. Now that I am older it is hard to believe Amma and Papa called him a boy. It's probably because he was a student teacher. His life would have been ruined. It is always the girl's fault if she gets pregnant.

It is also the girl's fault if she loses the baby. He stopped returning my calls when he noticed the swell of my belly. He did tell me first. We couldn't do it. He had too much to lose. And I had acted so mature when we met, he was so disappointed. I hadn't insisted that he put on a condom. It was my fault. It was decades ago. So much easier to leave someone and never have to deal with them or their bakwaas ever again. I didn't want to tell my parents who he was. And I am not mad at him for leaving, he was only at school for a few months to finish his training. He offered to take me, drive me three hours to take care of it. He'd even take care of me afterwards, we could lie and say I was staying with friends. He was raised differently. Why would my parents let me sleep over at a stranger's home? Because here, everyone is a stranger.

I looked him up. His dream came true, he became a high school teacher. He married a nice white girl. Has three kids with his now Queen (probably). I think they are ugly. I don't feel mean when I say it. I thought he was so cute and when I saw him, a little pudgy, a little bald, I couldn't believe I lost my future over him. Still, I am glad I didn't have his baby. It would have been bad. I wasn't ready. I'm an adult and I still can't take care of myself. Amma has always helped me figure it out, instructed me.

She'd be starting her 20s now. I know she is a she. I would have named her Tulika. I named her Tulika. I talk to her sometimes. When I have trouble sleeping. She gives good advice. I have trouble remembering it when I wake up though. I always mean to write it down before I drift away but never do. I have trouble remembering it when I wake up.

I didn't mean to cause the miscarriage. I wasn't throwing myself down the stairs or anything but I really didn't want to have the baby either. Tulika. I was really young. Amma and Papa never let me talk about it. The inevitable happened and I went to a psychiatrist. Things started to change. I learned that it wasn't a miscarriage. My doctor, I don't know why but I just can't remember her name after all these years, she said it was a stillbirth. It doesn't matter. I wanted to hold her but Amma said it was bad luck. I never saw her again. I don't know what happened. Tulika. It was better for everyone if I didn't ask. I didn't want to start another fight. We just all act a little more distant than usual on her birthday.

And still Amma and Papa did not mind bringing it up when they were mad at me. Or themselves. They said it was because of me. And how I was always yelling at them and being a nasty girl. Smoking and doing drugs. But I stopped as soon as I learned I was pregnant. At least by the time I was in my fourth month. I was an idiot kid. I regret so much of how much I fucked up. All for the attention of a stupid boy. Man.

But I have to be glad Tulie is dead. I wouldn't want her out there or in here with me.

It's time for bed. Tomorrow is going to be a long day. I ate very little of what was given to me so that I could eat more tomorrow if I was feeling weak. And more importantly, so I could ration for Day 3 if I didn't get a delivery. Every other day at 2:40am. That is the same time I can flush the toilet and wash myself using one of the two, small hand towels I packed. Amma was smart. She made me pack those too, I can't stand being greasy, feeling that my face is dirty. My hair will be the worst. I have to be sure not to take my braids out, I fiddle with them when I get bored sometimes.

Amma is smart. I was so mean to her. I thought I was smarter than her even though she was always smarter than me. She was practical. I had so many dreams and I never even thought to ask her what she had dreamed as a young girl. My dreams were selfish, they were all for me, instant gratification. Amma is so smart, I'm certain her dreams were not, they were for me and Raj, and now Abha. I don't know if she had dreams for Papa. He probably told her what to dream for him. That or they never discussed having dreams. She didn't discuss them with me. It's embarrassing to know your own mother doesn't want to get to know you. Doesn't want you to know her.

Her and Papa came here decades ago. They loved this country. She was glad my father was dead by the time Knight was elected. Raj and I were glad too. Papa would not have been able to hear the rhetoric that election year, much less fathom that we were electing a man who openly declared he wanted to be a dictator. Corruption is what my father ran away from. He despised it. Amma was used to corruption and bribes. Despite living here for as long as she has, she always assumed everyone was simply waiting for a bribe. She was right. I never believed her. I thought people were kind. I was really naive the whole time I was embarrassed of her. Of me.

How will I know to flush at 2:40am when I don't know what time it is now? Right now I know that it is past 8pm because my dim lights are on. My lights are only on 8pm until 3am. That's because there are no worker-wives here past 3:30pm. Well, they work from 7am to 3:30pm. They may forget something at their workstation and then come back. It's unlikely but it could happen. But they'd only have until 6pm to come back. So they should just plan to never make a mistake and leave one of their belongings at their work location. Trust their Knights won't steal or snoop. 6pm is when all women have to be inside. Safer if they aren't out after dark. They should be serving their husbands dinner soon after curfew so need to plan to be there before that. Cooking. Cleaning. Washing. Dreading. Making sure meals are on time.

If you don't have a husband, you may be assigned to one. They can request you if they notice you. Check you out. You may only have one husband to serve dinner to but the Knights, on a special occasion, maybe to treat their colleagues, escort wives to serve breakfast. And I've heard some wives serve meals like a food cart on their way to breakfast. That hasn't happened here though.

The stories I've overheard. When examples need to be made in other Knight territories. Terrortories. Knights can go to the canteen in Capital City too. I've heard that resistors and borderland vagrants are taken in from all over to 'work' there. That way a Knight has access to a loaner wife if he is in the city for a big trip and wants to make memories. If your Queen is working at the Central Home and Hearth, why not make a trip and treat yourself to something special? And all Queens take their cycle at the birthing center healing themselves if not helping another Queen through labor. Sending well wishes. Plenty of opportunity throughout the year to take advantage of your status if you're a Knight.

But how do you become a Queen?

Well, sad news ladies - you can't anymore. Marriages between a Knight and a Queen are only recognized if they took place before the nation's split. All marriages that took place after that had to go through a recertification process, Knight wanted to make sure they were valid under our new government. His new government. A marriage recertification which included The Knight's Right. Just in case you haven't heard of this, which is possible I suppose, the Knight's Right states that the highest-ranking Knight who owned the property that the husband and wife named as their residence on their new, valid, marriage certificate, had first right to sleep in the wedding bed with either newlywed.

There were people who didn't believe it was real at first. Amma advised correctly, immediately; *don't be stupid, reach out and bribe the property owner.* And of course at the beginning there were dear husbands who stood tall against the terror. *"There is no way I will let anyone rape my wife of three years.*

I will fight anyone who tries." That didn't last long as the law specified 'either newlywed'. How many dear husbands could stand that shame? Make no mistake, the Knight's message has always been clear: assimilate now, assimilate once we break you, or assimilate when you die. The choice is up to you!

I suppose it is a lie that I said you can't become a Queen nowadays. I'm sorry, I didn't mean to lie. I spoke too quickly again. Let me try to explain again. All men are Knights. All Knights are husbands. All women are wives. Only some women are Queens. A Queen is beyond a wife. She's the Queen of the home. A Knight's partner (and laughably his advisor) in ways than a worker-wife could ever be. A Queen is assigned to a single Knight. There are no love marriages anymore. I suppose a few remain but do those elder Queens really still love their Knights? Did they ever? I suppose they grew up at a different time, had fewer expectations of men than my generation pretended they could expect. It all happened so quickly that just like Amma they got to think to themselves, *'I was right'*. Life choices confirmed. When you choose living safely over living boldly, you have regrets.

A Queen cannot say no to the proposed marriage. It's up to the Knights around her to decide if it is a good match. And if she passes her virginity test, it will be a match. See, when you do things right and follow the rules, there's no need for The Knight's Right. Death before divorce. Unless you dream of becoming a worker-wife in a canteen. They'd probably allow that but they'd be so mad they'd have to decide which is worse. You'd be bringing such shame to your household. But it's out of your control if you want out. Your Knight gets to decide, you trust him to make a good decision for you I'm sure. Queens can't make the best decisions, especially without a Knight's guidance, they are a rare and precious commodity after all. Their perspective is off because of their sheltered lives and high status. Queens can only be married to a Knight once. Widowed Queens are given a special honor. Senior Queen. Their headscarves have crosses on them, so everyone knows to honor them. Their sacrifice and management of the hard-working worker-wives are what make everything happen. They are allowed to pray and read the Knight's scripture together. They can't study medicine but they can help with remedy in other ways. Breathe with you, sit with you. Take care of your little ones at the birthing center. They are not requested to be worker-wives. To even joke about a Queen in this way is a sin punishable by sealing your lips. It really is worth it to outlive your Knight. What a life! I suppose that's what I would try first, make the best out of the situation while we are here.

And you still don't know how to become a Queen, do you? It's hard to do but really, it's simple. Become small. Don't let anyone ever notice you. Don't ask to work outside your home. It is better to go hungry, with one robe to wear, never leaving your parent's home than to try to bring yourself out of that poverty and risk becoming a worker-wife. If you can make it to 15 without having gotten into any trouble, and your father is a Knight who holds high regard in your community, you will make a fine Queen. You will help build relationships and strengthen trade and travel routes if your town's Knight council is strategic as matrimonial offers arise. You don't get much say into whose Queen you are but you do get to say you are helping everyone so much. There are only a finite number of Queens and they do so much good for our Knights and communities. I told you they were a precious commodity.

It really is simple, if a woman cannot pass her virginity certification when she turns 15, she can never become a Queen. She is worthless.

"Momma, can we play spelling bee?"
"Shush darling. Let's practice spelling bee instead."
"But we never play until morning when we practice spelling bee."
"I know darling. I'm so sorry darling."

Chapter Two

I don't recall falling asleep. I just dozed off. I didn't think I'd be able to sleep in here. Even if there's nothing to do, it doesn't feel like it's safe to sleep.

There's something I've been thinking about. If anyone finds my Gamer Girl, how many generations will it be that the worker-wife who stumbles upon it won't know how to read my message? I think just one. Use it or lose it, they say. When they changed to home schools for girls, they also changed the Department of Education mandated curriculum. Well, before they entirely eliminated it. There's more important things than education right now. We are at war after all. So now a Queen can learn to read and write if her Knight allows it. Until then her curriculum is household studies. Whatever I decide to write, it needs to be short so they could memorize it. I'll use emojis but there are only a few to choose from. Worker-wives learned early on not to secretly teach their daughters at home. It's hard for girls to hide what they've learned.

Here's something else, and it was the strangest thing, my journal and pen were tucked neatly between the mattress and the wall, I don't recall hiding them there as I was falling asleep. I must've thought I was going to fall asleep on my Gamer Girl and crush her if I rolled over. I used to always place my glasses on the floor and slide them under my bed when I was falling asleep when I was little. That way nobody would step on them and only I could find them in an emergency.

I am Amma's daughter. And Amma raised me to think of the worst possibility first. Plan for the worst. Check and then double check. You don't know if the house will catch fire in the middle of the night. You don't know if you will get hit by a drunk driver if you walk home from school. And if the worst doesn't happen, accha. You don't know. You definitely don't know. She didn't know. But did she? She did. She planned. Right away, after the election results came in she told me, "Don't worry beti, we Desis always look out for each other. Especially around powerful white men." I didn't know what she meant but it made me even more scared. I thought of the worst, they were going to try to send us all back. Nobody would stop them. It didn't matter that we were willing to convert to Knight's sect of faith in order to stay here. Who would stop them if they decided we didn't fit in?

Luckily we were useful. Considered an established necessity in town. Amma's planning. Her convincing of Papa after the motel was found to be successful. Having the location so close to the motel helped Papa make his decision. So on her own, Amma ran The Chai House and made it a priority to be on extremely friendly terms with local law enforcement. When Sheriff Paulson ran for re-election he always did a photoshoot at The Chai House, Amma was so proud to be his face for diversity. It was embarrassing, everyone at school got those leaflets in the mail. Made fun of me. Amma was smart though. She didn't need a doctorate to know that she could help Sheriff Paulson look tolerant to folks who wouldn't usually vote for him. And if folks were hesitant, not fond of some of his strict enforcement, they felt better voting for the candidate who hosted community hours at the exotic Chai House; "He supports small business and immigrants! What a down to earth guy!" She didn't mind helping him because he helped her. Us.

Amma worked to create that relationship with Sheriff Paulson. She put signs up all over town, always ready to advertise specials for the community. Teachers got a free coffee on Teachers Day. Mothers got free flowers at our Mother's Day Buffet after Padmini came back to town. It was nothing terribly creative. But before we opened she let Sheriff Paulson know there would be a special for him and his colleagues no matter the day. All local law enforcement got a free sweet with their chai or coffee if they stopped by during their shift. Papa praised her for being so smart, "Free advertising, free security, no riff raff will mess with us or try to use the bathroom for free. All for the price of a laddu."

I hated it. When I was a teenager, I thought that the cops knew I was a nasty girl and that's why they would stare at me. I was paranoid, I always thought I was on the precipice of arrest, I was going to get caught for something I didn't even know I'd done, for being where I wasn't supposed to be. If that happened, then I'd have to put out as a bribe. I didn't have any money and I couldn't bring any more shame to Amma and Papa. I didn't know why back then, but I was right to hate the cops. They came in for free treats, not to protect us. They were monitoring us. We weren't one of them. Never have been, never will be.

In name Papa would have been a Knight. He and Amma were both US citizens. They stopped allowing new citizens the year the nation split and when Knight took over our terrortory, some citizens had to be sent back. Amma didn't have that fear. She'd always hush me if I started to say I was scared for her. No one from our community was sent back. Of course it was only us and Padmini left. The Kims left as soon as they noticed the fracturing start. Shortly after the Khans did too. I hope they are all ok. I wonder about them. If they're still here or not.

I think Papa would have died those first few years if he had been alive when Knight was elected. From a broken heart and because he was not one to be quiet when he saw stupidity. Even to Sheriff Paulson he would stand up. Let him know how smart he was. Just because he had an accent did not mean he was dumb.

There was absolutely resistance by men at first. Papa's family were freedom fighters back home, marching against colonial rule decades earlier. Our country supported their freedom back then, they would have marched with us in solidarity. That could never happen today. No freedom fighters left. There was too big of a pay increase, it turns out freedom is not free. The American men who didn't believe? Who wanted more? Something different? They never got to really fight against the Knights. It did not take much time for the new regime to begin arresting and eliminating men who would not follow The Knight's Code. Most military and law enforcement around here were Knights even before Election Day. It made everything very efficient.

A man speaking out against a Knight's Order? You are now off to do the hard labor of cleaning up the flooded and mold infested cities of the South East. You won't see your family ever again.

A man refusing to follow a Knight's Order? You are now off to do the hard labor of putting out the rolling fires out in the South West. You won't see your family ever again.

A man sabotaging a Knight's work? You are now off to do the hard labor of cleaning up the Mideastern wastelands. You will see your family in the hallucinations the fumes cause. You will never hold them again.

You already know what happens to any woman who tries any of those things. Sex gulag.

You know there are no Knights that escort you to the Mid-Waste? Can't risk the poison getting back here. Or worse, genetically altering a Knight so they can't reproduce with their Queen. It would be really bad if there were no more Queens for our Knights. They are our main currency. Our entire society is backed by them. They hold all the power and none at all.

We were useful to the Knights though. Amma couldn't be seen as running The Chai House of course. Raj took over. He's in charge of both The Madison Motel and The Chai House on paper. Raj took over The Chai House in name because he loves Amma. He hated The Chai House so much growing up that he got his Master's in Public Health and became an epidemiologist just so he would never have any reason to help Amma out. He would never be a Chai Walla. Nana and Nani shamed Papa so much about that. Papa was respectful and silent. He operated two businesses with his wife, seven days a week, 365 days a year. But to them he was just a Chai Walla, despite having gotten **their** daughter out of India. But it didn't matter in the end, none of it did because he made his first son, the holder of his legacy, Raj Saxena, into a Chai Walla. Raj tried to run from that possibility and all of the sudden it was the truth one day. Papa never knew though. I would never want him around to see us living like this.

Since Papa had died it made sense that Amma would go to the Central Home and Hearth to help the other Senior Queens in caring for the little ones and healing those Knights who came to them sick or injured. Except in those early days the Knights hadn't figured out how to segregate. If Amma laid children down for their naps and she was teaching those same future Knights and Queens the Mahabharata; they would not be able to remove those stories from those little minds. There was a Knight's curriculum for boys and girls of course, it's just that with those little ones, the Knights couldn't contain how Senior Queens soothed them. It was too delicate a situation. And one thing that was out of the Knights control. They aren't good with little ones.

So, if you are a Senior Queen they can't quite figure out how to control, they'll make an allowance if you have the right connections and can move under your son's roof. And if the Knights have no need for an epidemiologist but they do have a need for caffeine and a place to host their meetings, they may suggest what your best options are. Hard labor or Chai Walla, not a hard decision for Amma to push Raj to make. Raj really had no choice. He would never leave Abha like this. Alone in this world.

And so, like I told you, Amma was prepared. She followed the rules and was ready to adapt and follow the new ones. Her whole life, she had taken care of her family and herself. When it came to me, I didn't even know I was being taken care of. After I started seeing my psychiatrist I decided I wanted to become one. She helped me so much. I didn't share my dream with anyone. I didn't want to let Amma and Papa down. Chances were slim and it would take a long time. I took a college course online here and there. Nobody knew. And it took me so long to save up to pay for them, Padmini helped as much as she could. I would study in my room after everyone was asleep and I was done working my shifts. Amma and Papa didn't exactly pay me for helping them with The Chai House or The Madison Motel. I was getting free room and board after all.

—

Ok, that was so strange, it happened again. I don't recall falling asleep. As Amma says, my body told me what it needed. Luckily I at least have some light now. So probably only a few more hours until I get my next meal and can get a refill on my water. I didn't plan well there. I brought two full water bottles with me into the closet. I have been rationing that as well. Amma didn't want me to pack any food. She trusted Padmini to bring it to me. But I couldn't help being scared, what if she didn't? I have two of the snacks left from when I arrived. A granola bar (140 calories) and a bag of trail mix (330 calories). I think it's important to retain some normalcy. Just because the world is ending doesn't mean my anorexia is.

How dumb and difficult am I? In a world where every woman is a slut, that any man can call on demand, I can't stop obsessing about getting fat. My worth is still tied to it while I am currently locked in a closet, attempting to get smuggled up north, and am worried I will get fat because I am sitting or lying down 23 hours a day. I wish I didn't care. Nobody even sees me ever. This patriarchy will kill me one way or another. And I will never stop it. How could I?

Amma tried so hard to save me from it. She was so proud I was trying to go for med school. Even if I was too old.

"Beti, if you are a doctor you will never have to depend on any man. You aren't like me. I came here, didn't know English well. Had to cook, and clean, and help your father with the motel, learn how to handle this money, all while taking care of you. You know your father, do you think he lifted even one finger to help me?" she said, wagging one finger in my direction. Even when she was proud of me she had to dunk on me somehow. Remind me that I owed her.

I was still taking online pre-reqs when I found out my tuition was no good. It was only a few months after I had told my family I was trying. I needed more freedom, less time working at The Chai House. Amma doesn't like lazy people. She always has something she's doing, creating, working on. She says she can rest when she's dead.

After Amma found out I was trying to make something of myself, be useful to our family, she bragged, telling our family back home. We shouldn't have bragged. I shouldn't have told anyone. Kept it secret. Nazar lagna. I wonder if Amma thinks I caused it all, blames me too. I only had a few credits left before the election. Months of bragging, who knows who could have cast it. Someone who was jealous of our family's good fortune. I suppose we looked like we had it all. Looks are deceiving.

One of the first things Knight did was cut funding to all public schools, including higher educational institutions that had more women enrolled than men. My enrollments were put on hold. For just one year. I would be guaranteed one of the held spots for women next fall. For now, they had to offer my spot to a man or they wouldn't get federal funding for their programs, including medical units at the affiliated hospital. They had no choice. Patients would die. What a disconnect for me to be upset, if I fought it and got my spot, before I ever had my first day of class I would have killed patients. It was immoral of me to be selfish.

The Knights had a reason for their strict enforcement of withholding funds. We need to have more men working in society, in real high-end jobs, especially positions of power. It didn't matter that there were virtually no women in those roles at the time. It was Knight's fear of it happening. Maybe it was true. Our country was broken by women leaving the home to work. It doesn't matter the reasons why they chose to do so. In order to really fix things, we could not have our population rates of seven out of every ten women with a college degree and only five out of ten men with a college degree. Men needed those jobs in order to provide for their families. How could they even think of starting families with such low graduation rates? It was more important that women had the financial support of men to raise families. It doesn't matter if they were their families, we had to help one another out right now. Everyone should pitch in so we can fix things. Do we really want a society that needs both parents to be working?

While we all agreed no, there was a lack of creativity. For my whole life, there had never been enough to help families out so that parents didn't have to work. So they could be there with their kids. Help their families. There was enough for Sheriff Paulson to get more and more gear every year. For us to militarize our communities further and further. To install cameras in our towns to make sure we were safe. To build walls to keep us safe. To build prisons to keep us even safer. It was quicker and came at no cost (to them) to force women out of the workplace and into their homes. And they did it so quickly.

So, naively, for another year I looked forward to going to school. To one day becoming a doctor, helping other women. As a childless (kind of) unmarried woman, things stayed the same for me. Things may have even felt better. Is that bad to admit? I didn't have to study. It was tough though, lonely. They accessed our technology, it wasn't safe for us to talk to one another, we watched as powerful women who openly critiqued Knight online were sent away. They didn't want us talking to one another, teaching, creating, plotting, organizing. It was best to keep us isolated and it was easy to enforce. We were all so scared.

I continued my routine. I helped out at The Chai House. The motel was mainly Raj's domain. It made sense, it was mainly Knights using it; neither Amma nor I wanted to see why they were using it. We'd just come home to rest our heads at night and return to The Chai House as soon as we could. Raj wanted to spend most of his time there, running away from his Chai Walla destiny, working so hard at avoiding his reputation or at least making sure it was unearned. He was no Chai Walla, as if that was worse than his reality of becoming a Knight. In the end, whenever I saw him he spoke as though he hated us. And so we barely saw him, living and working at the motel, keeping the rooms clean and stocked for the Knights who had taken up residence there. We may not have chosen this but in those early days the pay was good. The protection was good. Sheriff Paulson made sure nothing happened to the motel or The Chai House. Participating kept our family safe even if we were not together as Raj worked to keep us apart.

So while I was one of the lucky few who didn't have an obligation to stay home to care for little ones or give up my jobs since I wasn't actually paid for my labor, there wasn't really anything to do with the free time on my schedule. My bad girl days had ended decades ago, I wasn't going to get drunk in the woods or look for boys to get pregnant with. I thought about what my psychiatrist would advise and I decided to use my time wisely, make change how I could. The time was going to pass any way so I would use it in a way that would benefit me and others. Maybe for the first time in my life.

I wanted to volunteer at the local community center to help folks needing mental health care. Handing out pamphlets, giving directions to shelters way outside of town, taking down all their names. It was as good a way as any to pass the time as I waited for my future to start. I was lonely and I was bored. When I was scared I self-soothed by reminding myself that I was going to be an amazing psychiatrist one day. But Amma didn't want me to work. I had to be wary of people who needed help like that. Whose families don't help them. There's a reason for that. In the end it didn't matter, the community center was taken over by Knights and repurposed. If folks needed help, they could just become a Knight.

So I stayed in the back of The Chai House. Every day thinking that one day, just after a few more days like this, I would be on my way to changing people's lives for the better, meeting and working with people who felt the same.

I was settled into a few months of my routine of hiding from reality when it was announced, shortly after my never-celebrated birthday, that public schools would no longer be allowing girls to attend. The class sizes had been too large for the boys to pay attention and there was no reason the girls could not learn at home from their mothers. Jobs for men continued to increase as the few remaining working women stepped back from their paychecks in traditionally caregiving roles such as teachers, nurses, and social workers. If you were a woman with a daughter, you could no longer work. Most non-profits like the one Amma would not allow me to volunteer at collapsed if they weren't already taken over by the Knights. Knight wasn't one for social services. More of a bootstraps guy, earn the help you are asking for.

It was shitty of me. Doing nothing. But if I had made any posts, fought back in any way, Amma, Raj, and Abha would also pay the price. I felt so bad for all those girls. Raj's little girl. Abha isn't my biological daughter but she feels like my little girl too. Tulika would have loved her. I imagine how much fun we would have had together, growing up.

She was two at the time. Abha. Abby, we call her now, when we are outside, around others. It's a matter of time before we mess that up. I felt so sad knowing she wouldn't be going to school but I didn't do anything. I was too afraid to march in the streets and like cowards, Amma and I convinced Raj to shut up and follow orders. "Don't bring any attention to our family beta," she told him, "At least we still have Abha in our home. How will we live if they take her from us?" I wondered if Amma would allow her to learn to read and write. If Raj wants her to learn, if they find out she can, it will be bad. None of us would be able to handle it. So, we hide her away. They know she exists but they assume that like them, we believe little girls should not be seen or heard. Sitting here in this closet, I guess we really do.

Amma must have foresaw the future. Raj was a single dad. He wanted to marry the love of his life. When he met Alesha in undergrad he didn't tell us. We knew something was up. Later, because he had kept it a secret, Amma and Papa didn't want them to marry. That is what they insisted, Raj fought them and they never backed down. "How can we trust a girl who hides like that. No pride, no morals," Amma and Papa tsk-tsked. They said it again and again, but I know the truth is that while Amma and Papa are old school, they would have been fine with her if she was Christian. But because Alesha was raised Muslim, they could never invite her into our family. It doesn't matter that now she was Atheist. "No morals, this one." Amma used to say, "You can't flip flop on Bhagwan." But I think it is because she was afraid. Nazar. She was worried what curse would arrive if people ever found out that she was okay with their relationship. Her fear caused her to do everything she could possibly think of to break them up. It didn't work, it only made Raj's life more difficult than it needed to be.

And through all this Alesha waited for him. She wanted to be with him, even knowing what his family was like.

Amma was prepared, selfishly so. She was so proud when she told Sheriff Paulson. They gloated together. Just like him, Amma had voted for Knight. Every day when he stopped by he was desperate to ask who we would vote for but always stopped short of actually asking. He must've been afraid of the answer. I saw how he felt his bond strengthen with her when he learned Amma voted for Knight. Knight did say he wanted to stop Muslims from coming into our country. Amma hates Muslims, and ex-Muslims too I suppose. The night election results were announced Alesha was done. Whatever Amma thought of her, Raj had to choose whether or not he wanted to raise a family with her. He'd already made the decision to create a family with her. They had been dating for over a decade. Amma and Papa's not-so-secret shame.

Who did I vote for?

Raj wouldn't marry Alesha but he would have a family with her in what Amma called *The American Way*. It made no sense, Raj showed us all exactly who he was and Alesha was blamed for it. I was so mad at him. I was so mad at her, why did she stay with him? Who cares what Amma and Papa said? They would absolutely accept Alesha if Raj would just stand up and marry her. What example was he setting for Abha? To watch her mother be treated like that. Raj gave Alesha money for Abha and would stop by for dinner a few days a week. Abha was too young to get to know him from a few dollars and hours a week. Whenever I brought it up, tried to tell him what a beautiful family and life he could have with Alesha and Abha if he just committed to that, Raj would dismiss me. He told me that he thought it was less drama for everyone, including Abha, to marry Alesha. 'She's more modern than you Swats. She doesn't even believe in marriage, I hear her counsel her friends in their, shittier than ours, relationships. She just wants to know we'll be together, which I am committed to. I am not going anywhere."

And so Abha continued to grow with Raj's occasional visits to Alesha's apartment, from what I know about men, likely booty calls. He was back to living at the motel but Amma always had him check in with us at The Chai House before ending his night. When the Muslim deportations eventually started, Raj did nothing. He knew how Amma had voted. Alesha was one of the first to go. She may have been born here but she wasn't anyone's Queen.

"I'm bored, Momma. Of spelling bee."

"That's ok honey, let's play numbers while we walk, you choose."

"Nines!"

Cindy knew her daughter would pick nines; it was also her favorite number to multiply by when she was that age.

Chapter Three

It happened again. I just kind of blanked out when writing. And same thing. Before I went to bed I seem to have tucked my journal and pen away. It's so strange I don't recall doing it. I woke up when I got my delivery. I ended up rationing my trail mix so I am actually building a bit of a stockpile based on the amount of time they said this would take; ten days tops. Then more travel but no more hiding in a closet.

But I should tell you how I got my food. And what I got. You want to know I'm sure. So much planning has gone into my freedom. It reminds me that I'm more important than I feel. How important I am to Amma. That she thinks I'm more brave than I really am.

Right outside my door is a painting. Behind that painting is a small cut out in my wall, a teeny window that they keep locked on the outside. I couldn't open it from here and I don't think banging on it would do much. The worker-wives would hear me. Maybe it would knock down Padmini's flower painting.

They come down in the witching hour, remove the painting, unlock the window, open it and lower a small cloth bag down to the floor. I can't say a word. They can't say a word. So, we don't. Amma explained all of this to me. I cannot afford to mess up. I do not have the luxury of hope. She told me that I can't ask for anything. I listened hard so I could hear their breathing. I wanted to say something to them, say thank you at least. Thank you for helping me escape. But I stayed quiet. My heart was pounding, vibrating through my chest so hard I was worried that they could hear it. I think I was trying to hear their breath, concentrating on who it was who was dropping off my delivery so much that I held my own. *We need to keep this all a secret or we will all end up doing hard labor.* I barely heard their footsteps retreating when they left. It could have been Padmini or the footsteps I heard could have been Jay's, it was hard to tell.

Next time, I will have the bag ready for them. I am only allowed to flush the toilet while that door is open. That is the only time so the bag has to be ready for pick up. We can't let anyone hear us. It's a check in too. The toilet flushing is the safest signal to let them know I'm still here and not decomposing. The real challenge is that I have to be awake every time they open that tiny door. I am worried I will miss it, especially since I seem to be falling asleep so easily, without even noticing.

On the back of the door to the painting is a tiny hook. I empty the bag and place it on the hook, that way it'll be ready just as long as I keep it there. Keep everything tidy and ready for me to escape, away from here. From all this.

This was all explained to me by Amma weeks ago. Be prepared. And then repeated as she watched me pack for my trip. I am aware of the consequences if I mess up. I don't get the luxury of hope. That they can just make changes on the fly because I made mistakes. Help me.

My bag contained a plastic bag which contained 4 individual frozen sandwiches, each wrapped in cloth. The plastic bag is for any waste and to return the cloths, all back to the inside the bag on the hook for pick up in two days. Until then, more solitude for Swati.

Frozen sandwiches, drinking water, and a glass jar with something so dark, thick and heavy I wondered if it was blood. I couldn't see in the dark but I could smell that it was Padmini's tomato juice. I was told to bring water bottles but I can't risk running out of clean water. So, I'll drink straight out of the jar. Anything left I'll use to clean up with before my next drop off. I may keep this jar. It would be easier to ration water that way. I hope nobody gets upset when I don't return it. Amma may worry what I could do with the broken glass, but I don't think Padmini would tell her. How could she? Why would she make her worry over a jar of water? There were also two pills for me. Multivitamins, they told Amma and me ahead of time. I would be in the dark for so many days, I had to make sure I was still up for the journey.

I haven't tried the sandwiches yet. They are still frozen. I kept three together and separated one out in the hopes that it would defrost a little quicker. Knowing they are giving me frozen food makes it harder to ration for the long term. Homemade bread goes bad so quickly.

They left me a note made using Padmini's label machine. *'One day at a time.'* I've been living one day at a time for decades now.

There was something I didn't like. Besides being locked in this very small, only sometimes dimly lit room, its decor consisting solely of a mattress and a toilet. I have been trying to stretch more. I felt warm air on my fingertips and noticed a vent at the very top corner of the room yesterday. The plate faces down. The ceiling is too high for me to reach it, but I thought maybe it could be a safe place to hide my Gamer Girl and message for Amma, Abha, or anyone else to find, so they know I tried to escape this hell. I want them to know that I love them more than I love myself, even if I only recently figured that out.

I know it was risky, but the lights were on so I knew that the worker-wives were gone before I tried. I know I wasn't supposed to. Someone could have heard me jumping. I could have hurt myself, rolled my ankle or worse. My thin mattress only gives me a few inches on top of my 5'6" frame. But yesterday, minutes after the delivery, I heard sounds coming from the vent. It was disgusting. I don't know if she delivered my food or if he did. I can pretty much guarantee you she wrote the note and packed the bag. If she delivered my food and then I heard those guttural sounds that is one thing. If he delivered my food and then I heard those sounds, that means I may not be safe.

Was he aroused at having a female prisoner locked in his home? Me? If so, it may take less than a week for him to just open the door and use me as his wife. He could never turn me in without facing repercussions. But he could use me as his rape slave. He is a Knight after all. There's no one left to save me but him. What would Padmini and Amma do to stop him?

I'm trying to calm myself. Remind myself of my safeguard. While I am locked in, I do have a very small amount of insurance that he wouldn't do that. After they opened the door and I walked into this room, they closed the door behind me, locked it, and nailed a pegboard over the wall. It takes a lot of effort for anyone to try to get me. Of course, there is nowhere for me to go even if I was able to unlock the door. I'll hurt myself and everyone else trying to get out of this sealed coffin.

—

I just blacked out again. How am I so sleepy? I don't know how long I was out. Even if I wasn't trying to preserve the Gamer Girl, the time only ever blinks 11:11. *Make a wish.* The date is broken too. Forever 11/11/1111. I couldn't have been out that long, the sandwiches are still frozen. The single one is cold to the touch. But I can eat it now. I am excited to report it is peanut butter and berries. I miss jelly so much. Papa used to always make me peanut butter and orange marmalade on the weekends. He loved peanut butter.

I have my dim lights. That means the worker-wives are gone. I imagine their reaction if I were to bust through the pegboard while they're working tomorrow. Do they have any idea? I know that if I try to leave I'd be putting them at risk. I know that if I were them, I'd turn on me immediately. Worker-wives need to protect themselves however they can. We don't fault one another.

I saw that pegboard when I entered the basement. It was just like you'd see in someone's garage. Except instead of tools, there were scissors, all different kinds. There were also hooks with three aprons on them. I dreamt of one day wearing a doctor's white coat and now I'm hidden behind three, calico print aprons. There are various sewing implements. Lots of string and clothespins.

Yardsticks. Misting bottles. Red embroidery thread. Lots of embroidery thread. For occasions when they need to get patched up. Or receive instructions to hush a Knight up. Make them a pussy. Those are always big events. Does Padmini feel honor or pride when she performs the ceremony? Between the two of us, I didn't ever predict she would be bold enough for that role. You've guessed it. I am writing to you from my home inside of your very own local Knight's apothecary.

I want you to know that I know I'm being too specific when I say local. If this all works out, no problem. But if somehow this journal gets found, all of Amma's planning is for nothing. I cannot risk anything happening to them and everything will all because I wanted to pass the time. To make sure I didn't go insane when I was locked in this room. Lose myself. But part of me knows, and I don't care if I sound crazy as I admit it, this journal is my legacy. I was meant for more than this life I've lived. What I've done until now is meaningless. People will know who I am and why I ran. Even if it is because I am scared. I need to do something about this.

I shouldn't think like that. It's too easy to go towards my dark thoughts. She'd remind me to focus on what I can do. But my mind goes back to thinking of what it will be like when I die. After I'm gone. And you'll find this and think, "*selfish girl*". I put my family and friends at risk just to make sure someone saw my ego.

But maybe you'll find this and you're trying too, helping someone like me to find her way to freedom. Maybe she can't read. At least you know there was a time when we could.

Maybe you're not a helper, maybe you can choose.

This journal isn't simply a way to pass the time. It is protecting me because I need Abha to know that I tried. That I am going to figure out how to rescue her. She can't grow up to be pregnant at 15. I must find a safe hiding place for it.

At least when it was me I did it willingly. Mark wanted me and I wanted to be with him. Didn't I?

It's scary for Amma, Abha, and me but I'm really worried about Raj. It's going to be toughest for him. Whatever happens, we're the immigrants. Sure, we were born here, but Amma immigrated. We need to prove three generations of citizenship otherwise Abha won't be a Queen. And we can't do that. So, until Raj has a son with a Queen (which let's be honest, they aren't exactly handing Queens out to Knights who are also Hindu single fathers) Abha will likely grow up to become a worker-wife. For now she would be safe, simply a worker in her father's business. But once her cycle starts, any Knight who wants, may claim her. So many rules. You don't even know you're breaking them until your neighbor is threatening to tell on you unless you give them a bribe.

Amma's protection from Sheriff Paulson has paid off for all of us so far though. He liked her because she gave him free stuff before she had to. She even voted for Knight without him having to convince her. She made him look like a nice guy. Feel like a nice guy. He may pretend not to see me but with Abby eventually someone will mention that she looks a little bit old to not be a wife. And even he won't be able to stop it unless Raj and Amma get some leverage with the Knights.

Do you believe that Amma so easily hid me? I was able to fade away. I didn't have any real friends to begin with. I was online a lot, but there was nobody in real life to hang out with. Once that was taken away from me, nobody beside Amma and Raj. Everyone in town had already started to see me less and less when I was studying. I was always in the back of The Chai House if I wasn't at the register. After being deferred from taking classes another year, Amma didn't want people knowing I was depressed so when she told me to take rest, I accepted her instructions. I didn't want to burden anyone with my existence. With my sadness. In my room, crying in the dark, I wasn't mourning the fact that I couldn't volunteer at the community center. I wasn't mourning for the protestors being murdered, for the neighbors killing one another. I was mourning my wasted life. I knew that women couldn't be doctors, teachers, leaders. It would never happen for me. We were needed at home to take care of the children. To strengthen our communities.

While our nation was falling apart, while our nation's leaders were escaping to their bunkers, the Saxena family was still ok. We weren't hungry, Sheriff Paulson always made sure our suppliers had an escort. For other families, food started becoming scarce as more people stockpiled. Younger girls were put in charge of their siblings as their mothers needed to breastfeed along with soak and peel and chop and cook the dried rations provided through the Knight's nutrition program. They didn't want us talking to one another, helping each other. They always found more ways to distance us. Women couldn't go shopping alone anymore. Knights could open up accounts at most shops for their Queens or select worker-wives that helped around their home and businesses. They made sure to limit our shopping hours and the number of people who could shop inside at a time as well, supposedly for everyone's safety. If we dared complain while the hungry waited for food the Knights would shame us, reminding us how lucky we were to be enjoying the nice weather as we waited in line for our *free* food.

The Knights at the grocery stores were some of the worst. They would accuse worker-wives with low status of shoplifting before taking them to a back room to search them. Even the most honorable Knight at the grocery store would take names down in order to serially wife women who caught his eye when shopping for food. They loved the power of intimidating women who were hungry, starving to feed their children. If they noticed a worker-wife buying something, they would check in about it with her the next week, making sure she wasn't helping others refusing to participate, doing another's worker-wifely duties. The system only works if everyone participates.

So, for most women, it was simply best to take the Friday rations. Everything you needed in one box.

Not too dissimilar to my rations now. Dried goods, rice, beans, winter vegetables that weren't rotten if you were lucky so you could make a stew to feed several until next Friday.

I remember Amma telling me a story when I was helping cut vegetables at The Chai House. A family was traveling home from visiting their Nani and Nana's and got lost when they tried to take a shortcut home. They eventually ran out of food as they found their way towards the trail leading back home. As they walked on, they passed a site full of tents, all claimed by performers. There were men charming snakes, women forecasting the future, jugglers, men and women doing the wildest acrobatics you could imagine. And the smell of delicious khana. The father asked one of the men if they would be willing to share a few small bites so that the children could complete their journey. If they cried from hunger, it was possible a thug or three could follow them and attack. Knowing they had nothing to offer the bandits, they would be killed. The man refused, with true remorse; there was only so much food for the performers, they had prepared for their journey and could not help today.

The family decided that as the day was nearing end, it would be safest to camp somewhere nearby the performers. That way, if something did happen, if bandits tried to hurt them, maybe they would be rescued. The performers didn't seem to mind. One of the jugglers had been throwing swords, how much of a threat could this one family be? The mother began boiling water. She had only a few potatoes. It would be best to dice them and serve them after boiling with some of the water. 'It will be filling but mostly water,' she worried out loud. Her eldest daughter came to her rescue. 'Amma, you make the best sabzi, it will be so, so good.' She reached her hand into her bag, pulled out a spice tin and handed it to her mother. 'Nani wanted to be sure we could trade if we needed to on the way home.'

Once the potatoes had cooked a little bit, the mother tossed some of the water and added several spices to her dish, mixing everything together as she fried the potatoes. Her son began cheering, 'Amma is making her world famous sabzi. She can feed everyone who comes to watch the performers. You watch, they will wait in line!'

At this some of the performers' perked up and began peering over to their camp. 'Arrey, you can try some!' the littlest child shouted, 'Come on over to try Amma's khana! Chalo!'

At this the man who had refused the family food earlier put his arm out to stop the performers from leaving camp. The family saw him frantically pointing and a tornado of bodies and plates and blankets swirled in the performers' camp.

"We could not enjoy your hospitality without bringing a gift for the host's family," the man said, not meeting Amma's teary eyes.

"Come, sit, and let's eat," the father said. The following day, the two groups, the performers and the family, left as one. The performers were welcomed by the family's townsfolk, where they entertained everyone and returned year after year to celebrate their new friendship.

That sort of thing would never happen here.

"Darling, hush!" Cindy grabbed Jenny's triceps, pulling her to her side. Jenny didn't whimper or wince in pain at her momma's correction. She instantly made herself small, hiding as much as she could into her, shoving herself into her momma's side. She felt her momma scoop her up and start moving quickly into the woods.

Cindy felt Jenny hide her face into her chest. Her entire adult life she'd been in combat and still considered her time at war peaceful compared to how Jenny was growing up. When she found a safe spot, she set Jenny down and gently tugged on her braids.

"Alright darling, we are going to do our fives now. Do you remember why?"

With her eyes still closed, Jenny recited from memory:

I breathe in
and count to five
I breath out
and count to five
I breathe in
to stay alive
I breathe out
and decide who dies

Cindy and Jenny counted their breath and then got in their tactical formation.

Chapter Four

I slept good last night. I ate the second of my sandwiches this morning. I think it was morning. It's always 11:11. I thought they were peanut butter sandwiches but the one this morning was potato and onion, just like my mom makes. Padmini remembers.

Her mom Lakshmi was good friends with Amma. She began living in India about half the year once Padmini announced she had married Jay. Lakshmi Auntie was furious that Padmini had eloped, she had been saving to have her only daughter's wedding in India so all their family could attend. After all she had been through, she could still finance her daughter's wedding on her own. But Padmini refused to participate in the culture. Thought it was bullshit that a wedding should cost anyone that much. Even though Lakshmi Auntie was angry about missing out on showing off, the timing worked out perfectly, or at least as perfectly as possible given the circumstances.

Lakshmi Auntie divorced Padmini's abusive father when Padmini was around ten or twelve. Padmini is a few years older than me, it's one of those things that seems huge when you're a kid but when you're over twenty-five it's no longer a thing at all.

I remember my parents getting weird. Padmini and I weren't friends as such, we were forced to hang out because of Amma and Lakshmi Auntie's friendship. Papa was a bit of a superstitious man; he thought their friend's marriage's problems would hitch on to Amma so he decided they shouldn't be friends anymore. He did not go out of his way to prevent Lakshmi Auntie from stopping by The Chai House, to place an order or say hello, but I noticed Amma didn't always tell Papa when she'd seen Lakshmi Auntie. She'd always take me with her. She wanted Padmini and I to be friends too, too much. Padmini didn't want to hang out with a little kid and I didn't particularly like Padmini. One of my friend's older siblings went to school with her and always asked if I was Pimply Padmini's sister. Did I eat with my hands too? Why did I take my shoes off so much? Pimply Padmini did that too.

Sometimes Padmini would come with her mom to The Chai House, sometimes not. I always preferred when not. Even though she was older, it felt like I was babysitting her. She would sit and read a book while watching me do

Chai House chores; washing dishes, prepping veggies, all the work Amma didn't really want to do. Raj was never asked to keep Padmini busy or really do chores. That's probably why he's so angry today. Imagine going your whole life never being asked to help and then being expected to do it all?

So, I helped Amma and babysat Pimply Padmini, future Queen Patron of Punishment. That way Lakshmi Auntie and Amma could gossip and drink chai. Padmini's father soon remarried, a good Indian girl. She was so beautiful. Meena. Now that I'm older than her I realize how young she was. How little she must've known having never really left her parents' home. And she moved to America knowing no one. She didn't even know her husband really. I don't think I could do that. What is her life like today?

I suppose the good thing about patriarchal Indian husbands is that they don't want to raise their kids. Like Amma always said, "They just want to tell everyone else what to do." Same thing with children as with their wives. They don't want to support them, just tell them what to do.

He couldn't stand not being able to control Lakshmi Auntie anymore, knowing that. Lakshmi Auntie no longer cared about making him happy. She had tried hard. She didn't want to feel his pain but there was nothing she could do that would ever make him happy. He hated himself so walked as though everyone else hated him too. Once Lakshmi realized that there was nothing she could ever do in this lifetime to save herself other than leave, she was out. She found help from other American women, not Indian women; she didn't need a crystal ball to see the judgement headed her way from them. She would rather be living with strangers than rely on her own husband for a single cent. They couldn't understand, how bad could it really be? Once he realized he no longer controlled her, that Lakshmi Auntie had friends who told him no, who couldn't be manipulated, who told him to his face that he should be ashamed of himself, that he was lucky he wasn't in jail, if he were their husband instead of Lakshmi's he would be in the ground, that his dumb ass should be worshiping the ground she walks on; he began to hate himself more and more. How dare those women speak to him that way. He'd control Lakshmi Auntie the only way he could figure, through Padmini.

When we got together, all the Indian families would gossip. There was one universal rumble at the time, even the kids were aware of it. All of the adults, the Indian Aunties and Uncles all frowned on Padmini being left alone with him. Even if Meena was there. Who hadn't heard of an evil stepmother? And once Meena gave birth to a son, Padmini wouldn't matter anyways. Lakshmi Auntie needed to take better care to protect her daughter. The whole situation was her fault and now she could barely take care of herself much less her poor daughter.

When they were together, Lakshmi Auntie's ex-husband wouldn't listen to her about anything that had to do with raising their daughter. He didn't want to be bothered by Padmini. To even spend time with her. He'd rather be seen for all he was doing. Once they split, he tried to convince everyone that Lakshmi Auntie did not know how to be a mother, how terrible she had been. She couldn't cook, couldn't clean, didn't help Padmini with her hair or skin. It was better if Padmini didn't know her, how her birth mother was being neglectful. Her new mother Meena oiled her hair, taught her how to do make up. All of the Uncles tried to reason with him, remind him how important it was for a daughter to be with her *real* mother. Especially at this age. But he didn't actually care about his daughter, he cared about teaching Lakshmi Auntie a lesson. He wanted her to remember that he gave her this life in America, and he could take it all away if he wanted to. She was lucky he hadn't taken all their lives.

He fought for full custody, for the daughter he didn't really, in any way, care about, and with equal disregard for his new wife and her inevitable battle with the women in our community who were never going to accept her. Lakshmi couldn't afford lawyers how he was able to. She was still getting financial help from the women's center. They had helped her with job skills and she had gotten a job folding clothes at Bergen's. A point of pride and also nothing compared to her ex's salary and career as an electrical engineer. She came into The Chai House so upset after she realized she wouldn't be able to fight. I was too young to understand, but I do remember being so scared that Papa would try to take Amma away from me. Papa scolded Amma when I asked him if he was going to take me away at dinner one night. "This is what I've been saying. Why don't you see how bad it is to hang out with that woman? Don't invite bad company into our home. It is always trying to sneak in. Do not invite it. How many times do you make me repeat myself?"

Padmini's father had the big house, the fun toys, a two-parent home for Padmini to invite her friends over to, the lawyers, he had it all, almost.

Padmini had gotten home from school early. It was one of those teacher's days at school. I was so young I didn't know the teachers still worked on those days. I thought just like us, they got to go home at recess. And so Padmini arrived home early, entering through the garage; from the mud room she heard Meena screaming.

I don't know what happened next. It's all gossip. Maybe she froze and waited. Peeked through a door to see why Meena was screaming. Maybe she walked right in and screamed *STOP HURTING HER*. Whatever happened, what she did embarrassed her father. "Brought him shame," I heard Papa tsk tsking to Amma, "Can you believe this nerve? Calling the police." Amma just kept sweeping up the kitchen floor when he said this. As if he wouldn't have killed himself or them both if they hadn't been able to dial 911. No one said to Raj and me, nobody should hit you this way. What they said was don't embarrass yourself by bringing others into your problems.

Whatever Padmini did that afternoon caused her father to absolutely lose it. Padmini's father took the belt he had been beating Meena with and hit Padmini. Accidentally or intentionally, the force was so great Padmini fell, landing on her face, her braces ripping the soft tissue in her mouth. When the Sheriff arrived - because although Meena was a good Indian girl, she was also a smart one and dialed 911 - there was blood everywhere. Padmini's father had been beating Meena for months. He was smarter with Meena than he had been with Lakshmi Auntie; he didn't give her permission or need to leave the house. No chance for her to make friends, for others to find out. But just like with Lakshmi Auntie, punches on the arm, screaming at her so she wouldn't ever have peace, hits to the small of her back (they're just kidneys, nobody sees the blood when you pee, that's your secret shame, worry, responsibility to fix), pinches, threats to ruin her family's reputation back home, pulling hair, locking her out of the house at night with nothing but the cotton sari she was wearing, accusing her of not loving him and blaming her for not. He didn't ever want her blood. No need for her to hide her beautiful face behind sunglasses. No one ever had a bloody nose. No one ever had a smile either. What do you think is the only way a pet will learn what's good for them?

I don't know if he beat Padmini or not. I'm assuming so. We've never talked about it but Papa hit us growing up. He used to hit me with a yardstick. I thought of that when I entered the room. Wooden yardsticks, hanging on the pegboard, ready to give Swati a swat. I'm sure Sheriff Paulson was fine with hitting a girl to get her in line. But when she's bleeding from her mouth, clutching her broken glasses, inhaling blood and tears as she sucked in her snot - Sheriff Paulson couldn't have that happen, it was an election year.

"I'm sorry Sid, there's nothing I can do. We can't drop the charges. I cannot be soft on child abuse. I need the women's vote." It wasn't until after I turned 30 that I realized Papa had been trying to help him. What did Amma think? Did she know? Was Papa hiding it from her? Did she suggest it? She always said we had to look out for one another just like the Americans did for each other.

And so, Lakshmi got full custody. Padmini's father gave up, got another job just far enough away. He didn't care to visit Padmini after what she had done to him. She should be ashamed of herself for ruining her family, getting her father arrested. She had been raised to hate men, he said, just how Lakshmi had treated him their whole marriage. Nothing was ever his fault. Just ask his mom. What a perfect boy he had been. Meena left him, went home to India. I'm sure she felt shame even though the shame was all her husband's. I can't imagine how she must've been shunned when she returned to her parent's home. Maybe she lied. And poor Padmini. Not only did everyone in school make fun of her for getting beat by her dad, but she was also teased when Brent Adams told everyone in school that he saw Pimply Padmini's dad picking up garbage with all the other criminals for his community service. Even though her dad was out of her life, he still made her life miserable. He proved his control. What would he think to know his daughter grew up to have more control than he could have ever imagined? That she was the one who arranged for Brent Adams to get sent to the mid-eastern wastelands? Brent probably didn't deserve that but he made Padmini's life miserable for years. She couldn't trust him, so it was just easier this way. Simpler to have him out of the equation.

Amma wouldn't have wanted me to know all this. Not because it was another family's private business. She loved gossip. The worse for someone else, the better for her to take advantage of. A ripe opportunity for her to be a hero when she brought food over and helped out, making sure everyone knew she was the one to rely on for truth and wisdom.

Amma tried to hide what Padmini's dad did from me because she didn't want me to learn that it could happen to me. What Papa did to us was because we were bad, we made a mistake, needed to learn a lesson. What happened to Lakshmi Auntie and Padmini was something else, but it was still their responsibility to fulfill their duties as daughters, wives, and mothers. They were being taught lessons too.

I found everything out from school. Because there were only two Indian families in our school district we had to be related. We must have been the same family. Why wasn't I laughing at their joke? Wasn't it *my* papa that had been picking up trash? Fulfilling his community service for beating my stepmom and big sister up. They all knew my mom ran The Chai House and for laughs would ask me if it was my mom with the funny accent who rang them up at Bergen's. I fought it. Corrected them. Until they broke me. I could take a joke so I made fun of myself. Started doing Indian accents. Telling them I would get high before the spelling bee and still whip their asses. It worked. By the time I got to high school I wasn't Indian at all. I did not want Indian anything. All I wanted was to be included as one of them, to be seen as white. I tried, I believed it and it worked most of the time. Until I didn't want that anymore. And then it was only because it felt too late. If Knight hadn't risen to power, if all the factions hadn't started, terrortories split up, if things had kept going, I'd still be doing the same damn thing. It makes no difference thinking that way because when I tried to come back to it, I think it was too late. The outcome the same.

"Amma, why didn't you teach Raj and me Hindi?" I asked her one night back then, after she had voted for Knight, before I didn't know girls wouldn't be allowed to learn the alphabet until they were married to a Knight. That it would be a skill for elite Queens.

Without even looking up from her chai her response was immediate, "Why are you asking me? Why didn't you want to learn?"

This is how it always is and how it always will be with Amma. Why didn't I do it right the first time?

Padmini went away to university. I think she even studied abroad for a semester or two. Lakshmi Auntie was so proud. She never remarried. Over the years she worked her way up to the C-Suite at Bergen's. All the way to the India division - there were a lot of clothes to be made and purchased by young women and girls in India and Lakshmi Auntie was beyond familiar with both sets of consumers. With Padmini at university it made it much easier for Lakshmi Auntie to leave the home she had fought to create. And everyone accepted that Padmini would be so busy with her studies she would only see her mom on breaks anyway. It made more sense for Lakshmi Auntie to visit her so that Padmini's studies wouldn't be interrupted. That was the whole reason she had come here in the first place. A better life for her daughter.

Amma hurt those last few weeks Lakshmi Auntie was in town. Papa was cold. To all of us, but most obviously to Amma. He was hurt by how much their friendship meant to Amma; he had no equivalent. No close friends to talk to. Just like me. Papa didn't fight but he instead went out of his way to make life a little harder for Amma, made her justify spending so much time away from both businesses and neglecting her duties as our mother. I was still young enough that I spent all my time outside of school with Amma, now I see how she held me close those months as Padmini shopped and packed for university and Lakshmi Auntie started downsizing. Amma and I helped her pack up and drove over to the women's center that had helped Lakshmi Auntie out so much, not so many years before. Lakshmi Auntie only recognized a few people that day and Amma and her talked about how good that was. It was a good sign that it was new women there, Lakshmi's former support network were all thriving in different ways now. Some of them had gone back to their abusive relationships but most had gone on to promising new lives. I'd never seen Lakshmi Auntie cry through all of her divorce dramas until that day where she got to donate her belongings to the place that had helped her through it all. When Papa would not even give her a motel room to stay in, instead working to convince her to go back home to her husband, these women moved her in that same night. Supported her as she worked to get Padmini into university and it was all happening. They were going to be ok.

Amma drove with Lakshmi Auntie to drop Padmini off at university. Amma promised them both that if anything happened, she would always be there for them. And she stuck to her word. If Amma says she is going to do something, Amma is going to do it.

When I was in high school, before I ever met Mark in English class or knew about Tulika, Padmini came home. Well, Amma left. We closed The Chai House, the only time it has ever happened. Amma didn't even ask Papa but just left in the middle of a weekday to drive to university and bring Padmini home. I came home from high school to find the closed sign on the locked door. I was too self-absorbed to care about what Amma was doing, just pissed that I could have snuck out to hang out with the cool kids which I never got to do because I always had to work. I didn't know I was about to spend my summer working overtime to hide Padmini's stay with us, I didn't want to be associated with Pimply Padmini after finally burying that part of me

Padmini lived at the motel with us for six months or so. I hate to admit that I never expressed care for whatever she was going through or why. She came back before my spring break and Amma and Papa drove her back to University in the fall. She worked at The Chai House and at the motel but Amma and Papa never asked her to. I was mad about that. For me, their own daughter, they demanded help. For a guest, living off us for free, plenty of time and space to help when she felt like it. I'm surprised I don't hate myself more. What a shitty person. To not even ask her if she was ok. And here I am, safe in her home, hidden from the Knights while she bears all the cost if found out. Making sure I got a comfort food tonight, through all of this. I wish I could say I would do the same. But I know I am so selfish. I think of me and my family first. I always think of me first.

Cindy was always so impressed by Jenny. She had taught her at a young age to be quiet, when to listen, when to interrupt, how to track, how to kill. Cindy was 17 when she had signed up for the army. Her own momma had signed a special form, an underage permission or application of some sort. She had been completely drunk at the time, called Cindy an idiot for wanting to get killed and demanded she put her down as the sole recipient on her life insurance policy: "Government property is expensive, don't be a dumb bitch." Cindy was glad Jenny would never know her. It made things easier this way. Cindy had never even written to her momma once she got out of basic. Others got care packages on regular intervals or on special occasions, Cindy knew there was too high a risk that her momma would send her lies, excuses, and the same sob stories she'd heard a million times before and Cindy would never be able to say no to helping her pay her bills. It was best to have a clean break.

"Momma," Jenny said quietly.

Cindy turned her head to see where Jenny was looking. The popcorn bird feeders were set on yellow strings today. It was time to turn around and move further out, Padmini was letting her know that no care packages from Deepali would be available any time soon. They'd travel out for three days and then back, they were running across less and less borderland clans nowadays but they'd still have to be safe.

Cindy kissed the top of her daughter's head as she plotted the rest of their route.

Chapter Five

I have one sandwich left. I don't plan on eating it. And I can't put it in the trash. I am afraid to rip it up and flush it down the toilet. If I am brave enough to try, I'm going to at least wait until after the lights come back on. After the worker-wives leave.

I ate the third sandwich after I finished my entry yesterday. A few bites into the sandwich - it was potato and onion again - I had strands of hair in my mouth, wrapped around my tongue. I wanted to scream but I had to stay in control. I threw it across the room, which here in this closet is two feet away, maybe three. When the lights came back on, I got on my knees to look at it. If I could see the color of the hair I would know if it was Padmini's or Jay's. Or maybe it was one of their worker-wives. I wouldn't know who it was if that was the case. But it was important to find out. Who was messing with me? And I could not find the hair. What the fuck is happening?

And so, I have one sandwich left and I am waiting for the dim lights to come on again. I'm not eating that blind in the dark. Once I can see a little better, I can peel the layers apart and find out. Use the dim lights and my flashlight. I've been taking the multivitamins. I think they really are vitamins. They have that chalky aftertaste. I'm so hungry. But I've been hungry before, it is my specialty.

Before Tulika was born I was a size 4. I was absolutely skinny and called myself a fat bitch when I looked in the mirror. Squeezed the fat on my hips. Hated the lines on my thighs. I knew nothing about hating myself. After Tulika was born I found myself wearing a larger size, which I now know is a normal size. At the time I didn't think so. Amma and Papa put me on the shot as soon as the doctors said it was ok to. I ballooned after gaining all the baby weight. In a matter of weeks I gained 40 pounds on top of my pregnancy weight. All that weight, I didn't care when I was gaining it. I'm getting hungrier thinking about it. Before I had been afraid to be fat. Moti. After, I fell into a deep depression. I ate all the fried food Amma would serve up. After the third trip to the mall to buy new jeans Amma said enough was enough. Customers didn't want to see a moti girl, they would stop coming, think the food would make them fat. And "log kya kahenge"? Couldn't I ever just think about her and Papa?

People saying they are raising such an unhealthy girl. Didn't I ever want to be married? What kind of husband would I get?

Amma signed me up and took me to Weight Warriors. Made sure that I would attend, drove me to meetings, four times a week. I had a Warrior Buddy. She was probably a little older than I am now. Imagine stubborn, 18-year-old me. I was so obnoxious. We had to go over our diet journals and announce our weigh-ins at every meeting. My Warrior Buddy never lost a single pound. I don't believe her journal was accurate. But being right doesn't justify being cruel. I know that now. She sobbed when I accused her. I lost it one meeting. I screamed that she would be losing weight if she was eating only what she recorded. They matched her with a new Warrior Buddy. I was rebuddied with one of the Weight Warriors facilitators. It didn't matter. I got back to a size 4 before my 21st birthday. Amma was proud and did not say so. Would just make comments, "Look, now you have such a nice figure, not like before." Before being when I had a belly the size of a county fair award-winning pumpkin? Yeah, I had a better figure than before.

Wanna know my secret? I discovered running. Did you know you can burn up to 100 calories running just one mile? Did you know that if your parents are ashamed of you for getting fat and you cannot stand to be in the same room as them you can just lace up your shoes and run away as fast as you can? I never paced myself, all that mattered to me was how fast I could run away. I could run six miles and then eat 1500 calories and still lose weight. And my sleep. I have never slept so well my whole life. I was so tired all the time. When I went to bed I no longer heard Tulika's cries, the cries of my phantom daughter.

I finally got down to a size 0 when I started seeing her. Once I got the prescription for Phennies there was no stopping me. I could run further. I helped Amma and Papa more - with no anger towards them. I was able to go to the local community college. I was making Amma and Papa proud. I slept ok. Sometimes, if I stayed up too late studying I would see a little girl, playing games, laughing as she did. She'd run past me in the corner of my room. It was the stress, and starvation, and sleep deprivation. It was going much better still for me though. Better than it ever had. Amma's doctor friend had saved my life. She grew up like me, she understood how Amma and Papa were. But she could not rescue me.

Amma and Papa were so proud of what a good Indian girl I had become. I felt it. They felt protective of me because I tried to meet all their expectations. I earned their safety. I earned their love and protection. A few times a year Papa would field phone calls from relatives from India. An acquaintance had a son. Papa had a daughter who was almost 30 and still lived with him. Who didn't graduate college, didn't work. Surely he would want to get rid of his problem. How much would it cost for his daughter to be married off to a family who simply wants roots in America?

No one could pay enough. Papa always delayed a response when they tried to arrange visits for us kids to meet. He didn't want his daughter marrying an Indian man, which is also how Lakshmi Auntie felt about Padmini.

When Padmini graduated from university with a Bachelor's in horticulture, she moved back home. I was amazed. I thought she was stupid. She could have gone anywhere in the country, the world, she wasn't tied down with her mom being in India most of the time. But she had an idea. Staying with us that year made her realize she could either work for someone else or work for herself. So, I don't know how she did it, but she bought a small farmhouse, all the way on the outskirts of the other side of town. You had to drive almost two miles up her driveway before you got to her house. In winter, she stayed home. Truthfully, she almost always stayed home. She put her horticulture degree to good work, using what she cultivated to create tinctures and potions. She got huge exposure when her lavender sleep tincture made it onto Shay Matley's list of 100 favorite stocking stuffers in her *Put Christ back into Christmas* edition of her livestream. That was years later of course.

The important thing is that she knew that would happen. She manifested it. When she bought that farmhouse, she did it on her own. She had a scrubby boyfriend move in with her. I think they met online when she was at university. I don't know what their relationship was like. It doesn't matter that he had been famous for a while as a kid - as an adult, he was gross. Amma and Papa thought he was using her. They didn't see him at first, only saw him when Lakshmi Auntie asked them to check on Padmini. It seemed that Padmini was hiding something from her mom. When Amma and Papa finally went over as a safety check on behalf of Lakshmi Auntie, Padmini pushed him aside so they only ever saw his face from a distance. They learned that he was former child star Jay Harwood a few weeks later.

Amma could only report back to Lakshmi Auntie that Padmini was just fine, she had had a friend over so they couldn't stay long. That burden was off Amma. Lakshmi Auntie could now ask her daughter directly about her visiting friend. The morning after that visit, the phone rang as soon as I flipped the open sign on the door of The Chai House. I didn't answer it. Amma had been at the till so turned around, grabbed the phone, and kept repeating, 'Accha', or 'Then come over then, you know I'll be here all day.' - all while counting out 4 singles and 1 dollar in exact change (*2 quarters, 3 dimes, 3 nickels, and 5 pennies, do not mess it up Swati or dinner will be late*) to inspire people when they noticed the tip jar. “Nobody puts money into an empty tip jar beti”.

And within the hour Padmini walked through the door of The Chai House. Amma gave me no instructions so I stayed. Padmini ordered and I started making her a drink. Amma sat down at a booth and waved Padmini over. The Chai House is small. I heard everything. Jay was like her. They had gotten to know each other so well, staying up late to talk. She didn’t mind that he lived there for free. She wanted to take care of him, just like he took care of her. He loved her. Could Amma imagine a former Bollywood star falling in love with her? Boring, plain, father-who-never-loved her, Padmini? Amma didn’t understand. They could love each other without him sleeping in the same bed. They weren’t married. Padmini had no security. Jay could get her pregnant and leave. And there’d be nothing Padmini could do.

“Love schmove,” Amma said, “Don’t get pregnant. You’ll be stuck with him forever then.”

“You don’t have to worry about that Deepali Auntie.”

“Yes, I do have to worry about that, what will your mother say when she finds out you are living like this with a boy?”

“Auntie, she understands, she wants a love marriage for me. She knows. His father was the same. His mother never left. He is a good man. He needs help and I love him and will always help him.”

“You are making a mistake. Men only ever want one thing. What is he bringing you?”

“He’s different.”

“Then we will have to agree to disagree. Let’s drink our chai, what mint did you bring me?”

Why did Padmini even try to explain? What would Amma have possibly done? Told Lakshmi Auntie, “Oh don’t worry, she loves him, everything will be fine.”

And it doesn’t matter because eventually Jay did win everyone over. He really is a good guy. For a Knight.

Cindy was starting to worry about food. She always worried about food. They had a few potatoes, carrots, and onions left but they had to keep moving. During the day they slept and at night they moved. She couldn't exactly set up a campfire for stew, it would take too long, and could attract some of the borderland clans. As she watched Jenny take a break to stretch, looking up into the trees, Cindy thought how she had really lucked out with her daughter. Jenny was a natural, if you looked at her you'd think she was simply stretching. Cindy knew this was one of Jenny's preferred signals, she loved being able to tell her momma to follow her lead.

Cindy walked over to her. Jenny exclaimed she was too tired to walk any further.

Cindy scooped her up and whispered into her hair, "If anything goes wrong, you run."

"Three," is all Jenny quietly whispered back.

Cindy didn't have to walk much further before the three men accidentally stumbled across them.

"Please don't hurt us," Cindy whispered, slowly lowering her daughter to the ground.

"Oh, there's no need to hurt anyone, no need for any pain," a man of the borderlands leered. Cindy would kill him first. She could tell he was the leader as she stood in the woods with them. Two ex-Knights and a man of the borderlands against a woman and her young daughter.

"C'mon man, they're probably just hungry," one of the ex-Knights said to the leader.

"I'm hungry too," the other Knight spit towards them after he said it. And then he was clutching his throat. Blood poured through his fingers. Jenny decided who she wanted to kill first and beat Cindy to it.

So, Cindy charged her kill.

Jenny didn't mind if the nice one felt pain. Cindy watched as Jenny slid and sliced the hamstring of one leg and the calf of the other. Cindy brought her attention back to the man she was strangling to death. Her momma had taught her to always look someone in the eyes when you hurt them. To do otherwise was disrespectful. That is how we feel things together.

The nice one was begging Jenny not to hurt him as he tried to crawl away on his belly. That he hadn't wanted to hurt her. Jenny looked at her Momma. She wasn't supposed to kill but Momma was still killing. So, she walked behind him, she would make sure he wouldn't get too close to the road. But when she heard her momma's footsteps she couldn't contain herself, she skipped ahead and grabbed him by the back of his shirt.

"You lied. You wanted to hurt us, I see your shirt," Jenny said as she held him by one ear, pulling him back towards her momma.

"Now baby girl, don't play with them, you know that," Cindy corrected her daughter.

"I'm sorry Momma," Jenny said.

"It's ok darling, you thought you were right. Now go on, you can ask him."

"How many worker-wives did you have?" Jenny asked the ex-Knight.

"Wh-what?" He stammered.

"Answer the girl," Cindy commanded, kneeling before him, pointing the tip of one of her many blades directly at his eye.

"How many worker-wives?" Jenny repeated herself. That made her mad. Momma doesn't ever like repeating herself.

"I don't know. Twelve? Twenty?" The man sobbed, "They made you. They made me."

"Well, look at that now darling. You were right. Go on." Cindy nodded at her daughter encouragingly.

"Well, what do you say now?" Jenny asked the Knight. Ex-Knight.

"I. I'm so sorry," he cried quietly.

Jenny looked up at her momma.

"That's all he can do now darling. Be sorry for being a rapist, piece of shit," Cindy said apologetically to her daughter.

"Please, no," the man sobbed to Jenny.

"You decide honey," Cindy said to her daughter, "You can take some time."

"I'm doing it!" Jenny exclaimed as the Knight screamed no, quick to silence him as she stabbed the left side of his neck repeatedly.

"OK, sweetie, that's enough," Cindy stood up, "Time to see what they've got."

Jenny was happy, apples and peanut butter. It couldn't have been a more perfect reward for this fight. They'd be able to have some good snacking over the next few days, Cindy was happy about that too.

She couldn't stop thinking about it though. She was getting older but somehow the fights were getting easier. It couldn't just be Jenny's assistance. She thought they were always so slow now. How close had they gotten before the men thought they caught the two sneaking past their camp? They must be using stronger and stronger flowers from Knight. From Padmini's greenhouses.

"I wanna play constellations tonight Momma!" Jenny danced ahead of her, unaware of her momma's thoughts.

Chapter Six

I'm worried. I'm losing time. I don't remember sleeping. I'm worried I'll miss my next drop off. I'm going to try to stay wide awake. That's the only way I won't risk missing my drop off and the worker-wives run no risk of hearing me. I don't know what I'm doing when I sleep.

What if there were instructions that Padmini and Jay didn't give to Amma? Amma did not always tell me everything. She just wants to keep me safe.

It's going to be hard staying up for so long.

Maybe they didn't give instructions to Amma because they secretly want me to get caught.

It's a good day to start staying up all night. I have a delivery today. I haven't had a problem with the food since the hair. I haven't been really hungry though either. I love when that happens. But even when it does, I can't help thinking about food.

When I was really little and had trouble sleeping at night, I'd hold my breath and count. See how long I could hold it. How high I could count. A few times I counted so high I was able to see stars, like in cartoons when the character gets hit in the head.

I can do that with food too. I bet you can't guess how many hours I can go without eating. Let me know if you consider this cheating: when I was losing weight, I'd chew on my supper, spit it into a napkin, and put it in my pockets. In my socks. I'm sure Amma knew. I'd get up, go to the bathroom, flush it down the drain and then do it again after helping to clear the dishes. She knew and all I ever heard was how lovely my figure was getting.

It was so nice when I got the Phennies. I didn't have to pretend any more, *'I'm not hungry Amma.'* had an automatic acceptance, *"Accha beti but at least have your chai."* And I absolutely did (160 calories). That was beyond enough to make Amma happy.

That summer though, I think I was still fat. When I say fat, I mean I hated myself. I was a size 8 when I met Jay. I think I had one miniskirt I could fit into that was a size 6. I kept it in my bag and would change in the woods along that longass driveway. Just like Mark, he was too old for me. I was still broken; I wanted his attention even though I knew Padmini loved him. I had heard her cry to Amma how much she loved him.

And I didn't. I wanted to steal him away from her though. Feel better about myself. It took me over ten years to figure that out. And now I'm hiding in their basement. Amma would never have been so kind to me. And Amma never knew. I didn't tell her. I waited with shame for Padmini to use it against me and she never did. Instead, the fear and dread of it happening hung over me for years. Until Amma told me, "I have a way to get you out of here. And then you must save Abha." When I found out the plan, I froze. She had paid tens of thousands of dollars to people. Bribes. She told me that part of the deal is that Raj has to turn a blind eye to upcoming changes in worker-wife laws, something new that would now be allowed on the full moon. Raj isn't turning a blind eye. He's allowing Knights to gang rape innocent women in our parent's motel. All so I can rescue Abha. And I didn't tell Amma there was a problem with her plan. That I was the problem with her plan. I didn't even lie. Right before we left I could have backed out. I could have told Amma that in my gut it didn't feel right to hide at Padmini's apothecary. But I was too scared to even do that. Too scared she would stop loving me. That she wouldn't even like me anymore.

So now I'm willingly trapped in the basement of someone who would have every reason to cast nazar on me, on us. Padmini was jealous of Amma caring for me that one summer. I remember. And then I wanted to steal her man. In front of her.

And I walked in the door and let them nail it shut behind me.

"I love playing constellations Momma!" Jenny said as they began their walk, the sun setting quickly tonight.

"I know you do darling," Cindy replied.

"North Star race tonight Momma?"

"Sure darling, no shouting though."

"I know that Momma."

"And what else?"

"Just because we're up North doesn't mean our work is done. North isn't our destination."

"That's right darling," Cindy smiled at her daughter, "You're so smart, that's just one of the reasons why I love you."

Chapter Seven

If you were a man, how long would it take before you noticed your girlfriend's ONLY friend wore the same exact miniskirt every day?

I can tell you that for women, or at least us Desi Ranis, we notice on Day 2. We say something on Day 3.

"Swati, what's up with the skirt?"

I couldn't explain to her that it made me feel skinny. After being told what a useless fat daughter I was, this size 6, denim mini skirt made me feel like I was beautiful. Cool. Desirable. Not even in a sexy way but in a 'I'd want to be her friend way'. I was desperate to be popular in this shitty town. Bored. Damaged from being forced to give birth to a baby I didn't want and was too young to understand that what had happened to me wasn't all entirely my fault. So, I tried to do it again.

"It's just my favorite right now."

"I can't believe your Mom let you wear it out like you've been doing. She would hate for people to think y'all were poor."

"I think she's proud I can fit in it again." Once I said that, she dropped it. She understood. The motiphobia in our community is real. It was a lie when I said it and I didn't know what she understood. That the only pride my mother would feel is over my being skinny, or the truth. When I found I could fit into my old skirt again, Amma told me to throw it out.

"No one wants to see your cellulite. Stretch-wretch marks." she had said, shaking her head in disgust at me as she unnecessarily hand washed the dishes.

I think she was more disgusted seeing my fatness than she was learning that I was pregnant by a boy who I had made vanish.

I got a treat today in my linen bag. Popcorn. Someone packed up a jar of it for me. That was one of my favorite snacks. Salty, buttery popcorn (600 calories the way I like it). It was a little stale. It could be left over from The Sewing. I wonder who it could have been.

I was such a bitch to her and she was always so kind. We had lived together that summer and I had never gotten to know her. That first tour of her place, I learned so much. She greeted everything.

Hello Aloe plants. Thank you for healing us when our skin is burnt, or we feel inflammation.

Hello Mint plants. Thank you for brightening our smiles and breath, thank you for flavoring our teas.

Hello Sunflowers. Thank you for brightening my day and allowing me to roast your seeds.

So, when I say I wonder who it could have been, I definitely do not mean Padmini. Who had insulted a Queen? Padmini gets to be in a better spot than the first row. Padmini was the one who obviously did the actual sewing ceremony, Queen Patron of Punishment and all. Part of her duties are the refreshments. She's well known for her lavender tea. The worker-wives enjoy it as she works. The one time the Knights have to serve them. They still intimidate them. Most worker-wives come to make an appearance and the free refreshments are definitely enticing. Knight's son came up with it, to encourage folks to come on down, see what threats await them if they mess up in just the right way. Lavender, honey, and hot water. Free popcorn. "Come on down folks. The weekend is here."

They would have set this aside for me. She must have set it aside for me. There are rarely leftovers at The Sewing.

She doesn't sew them here of course. What a twist that would be! Amma wouldn't have agreed to any of this. And Amma can't predict the future. None of us can.

Padmini's property couldn't compare to Gallows Park. Gallows Park is a relatively new name. Like within the last year. Just one day, we all knew to call it that. There was no sign or anything, still isn't, but I don't know if that means there never will be. It does mean though that I get to see how long it takes before no one but me remembers it used to be called Barrows Park.

It's still used for vendors. Our town was built around it. Vendors from all over would come to sell their goods in their wheelbarrows. That's why we've been able to continue doing so well through all this. Amma has shared stories of towns very close by that don't end up getting their nutrition rations. They have to make their way from Gallows Park all the way back home. Pay off anyone they come across on their way through the borderlands. If you see a group of performers camping out, you are going to wind up dead. No amount of Amma's sabzi can save you here. Travel in great numbers and travel with a lot of weapons. It's likely you'll lose men.

That's why Raj's acceptance of full moon pleasures is sure to bring in a lot of wealth for all of us. We get paid a lot so these men can have a lot of fun -

just in case they die. It's the least the women could do. They get to eat for free after all. No one should ever get anything for free.

There's a stage in Gallows Park too. We'd have all of our festivals there. The county community theatre would always do a Labor Day show for us. It'd be sold out all three nights. Everyone would drive in. My whole family got all of our American pop culture from the stage in Gallows Park. *Grease. West Side Story. The Music Man.* And unfortunately, the one and only time I've experienced *Rocky Horror Picture Show,* it was there with my parents. Our last show we got to see with Papa was the hip hop hit *Lincoln*. Padmini and Jay joined us. We laid out our blankets together. Shared what was inside our picnic baskets too.

I've never been when Padmini is on stage.

The night was quiet and cold. Jenny had more questions about the constellations than Cindy could answer. Cindy wished she could get her a book. She wanted her to know more than she did, give her more than her own momma had. But it'd be damn near impossible to find a book out here.

Chapter Eight

Would you believe me if I told you that I've never eaten meat? I bet it's hard to believe. Especially nowadays, you know how it is. But that's why Amma's been doing so well. Why The Chai House is still such a hub. When Knights come to The Chai House, they know exactly what they are getting. They can see their food, what vegetables it's made up of. Even if it's fried, which the majority of Amma's menu is, once you take a bite you know it's an onion. Or potatoes and peas.

The Knights are able to get meat. I know they eat. And they joke about what it is. In addition to those very important educational changes to lift men up in our economy, one of Knight's top priorities, for his first 100 days, was to loosen food safety protocols. It was no longer necessary for meat to go through any sort of inspections or certifying processes. In order for businesses to thrive, we needed to trust that the leadership in these industries were the experts on what was best.

How early on did McCullough's Hog Farm know they had a mutated version of the flu virus? I'm sure the poor hogs had to be sick, but of course, their lives weren't worth anything more than profit to the McCullough's board members. So, they hid it. And a lot of people got sick. Not just their workers. A lot of people ate that meat. Knight tried to help. He personally had an ad campaign, telling folks to stick with beef and poultry until they could get all of the pork recalled.

But true patriots didn't want to give up eating pork. It made them feel disloyal to their country, and nothing the Knight or McCullough families did or said would make them stop. So, some decided to go out of their way to show how loyal they were, having their pig roasts and ham and pineapple pizza parties. Anything to stick it to the Muslims, show their allegiance to Knight by going beyond doing what he asked for.

Knight never banned pork. Or fined McCullough's. He didn't help the thousands of families who died from the hog flu or those who were permanently disabled due to the neurological damage caused by contaminated meat.

Instead, it became a loyalty test to them. Whatever doesn't kill you, makes you stronger. Right?

But you know that Knight's always here to help us. He's our savior and more. There was a pharmaceutical company that had been testing lab grown pork. All different types of lab grown meats and proteins in fact. He had production going and distribution rolling within six months. Sheriff Paulson, through one of his many connections, got a caseload right away, before distribution was available to others.

Amma accepted a can. There was no way any of us were going to eat it. We could have traded it within weeks for a bit of money. Amma half lied when the Sheriff asked if we had enjoyed it. "*How did Indians cook it anyway?*"

You've probably picked up that I'm not exactly the most worldly person. I haven't left my town much. I've gone out of state for school trips and stuff. I would have had the opportunity to go to Europe in high school and opted out in order to leave town to have Tulika. Amma never wanted to go out to eat. We had plenty of food, no need to waste money.

And so, I've only eaten Chinese food once. It was the first time Papa had to take me to the city for my recommended treatments. He probably knew Amma wouldn't have approved. I was still in Weight Warriors. Amma didn't want me eating out while she was wasting money on that. Khana from her kitchen or no khana at all. But I didn't have to attend meetings that week. The clinic recommended I stop recording in my food journal while I tried treatment with them. It all worked out that it was the day to try something new.

Papa was proud though. He was softer than her. "Beti, this morning may feel rough to you. I think we should do something that brings you joy before you get checked in. When I was a little boy, I used to love this Indian-Chinese shop my Mausi would take me to. I just know you'll love Chinese food; I want you to try. I miss that shop so much; my BIGGEST regret is never bringing your Amma there. You know I have been trying to convince your Amma to add a dish or two to the menu. We could even do like street food, and have tiffins ready for the deputies who come in all the time. They can bring them back next day and you can clean them. No work for them, you know how lazy those sheriff boys are. Just drinking chai when they are supposed to be working with my tax dollars. Beti, I thought that would be something you could work on. Amma doesn't want to change the menu, you know how she is. I haven't had Chinese food in years."

It went on for a while. I never agreed, I doubt I said anything. Part of why he spoke so much was because it was an effective silencing tactic. Patriarchal consent to his monologues. I was very used to Papa talking at me. I didn't have anything to contribute, he knew everything. He told me he knew me better than I knew myself.

I met my care team that morning. I watched as Papa was told to not come along with me. If I needed him, they'd get him for me. We'd already discussed that. He had a room booked for the next few days in case anything went wrong. He had a friend in the hospitality business so he would get to stay for free, but he was a good guest and had already packed so many gifts and would be taking their whole family out for dinner. He'd okayed it with the medical team that the two of us could go out to lunch before the rest of my stay. They said it was a good idea to eat something that I really wanted. I had been reporting having no appetite. It was good I was feeling hungry again.

I don't remember much about what they did that morning. I remember them asking if I was sexually active. There was a therapist in the room. She gently let the tech, doctor, medical assistant know to review past complications in my chart.

The checkbox next to SLUT was checked yes. With a line that said, "killed her baby". I don't know, I never went to med school to find out how they write in charts.

There was a ridiculously cute boy there. Man. They never left him alone in the room with me. Is that normal? Or did they know how I had seduced Mark? He would compliment me on something and then I'd do more of it. He'd always tell me how exceptional I was. Ask me who my boyfriend was. What was my story? I was fascinating, he wanted to know it all. We didn't have to do anything, only if I wanted to, he'd say. I knew the situation. He didn't want any trouble. He just couldn't help but feel this attraction to me.

When I was reunited with Papa, he took me to the spot. *The Panda in the Pagoda.* Being the daughter of a man who named his Indian restaurant *The Chai House,* I wasn't surprised at all. I'm sure he had already arranged it with his friend.

Papa did eat meat. Amma hated it. She thought he should feel shame. He should worship all life as she did. If he didn't, what respect could he have for her? Papa didn't care. He was in America and if he wanted to have a cheeseburger on the 4th of July with Sheriff Paulson, no one would stop him. Especially not five-foot tall Amma. I have no idea if it was worth it for him or how often he did it. He was a smart man. He could get a slice of pepperoni pizza at Sal's or chicken wings down at Catty Sports Pub. But if Amma saw he had been eating meat, she would force him to wash everything. If it had touched a plate, a utensil, a pan, even the sink those items had been in, along with the clothes he had been wearing. I'd see her disinfecting his steering wheel after he had started his shower. Raj and I would hide. If we were seen OR heard there would be a beating. Tip toe to your room, sneak the door shut; do not let it click. Once we weren't quiet enough and Amma smacked Raj in the ear with Papa's belt; *"turn off your light and get under your blanket."* I was older when I realized I could be under two blankets and read with a flashlight without getting caught. As soon as I heard the footsteps I'd pretend to be asleep.

Do you know why Amma beat Raj? Because he was the closest she could ever get to beating Papa. No matter how hard Papa would try, I would never eat meat. Raj would go to those grill outs with him. But with me, no way. He'd try to get me to eat those pizza slices, wings, and burgers. Try to trick me, putting it in sauces or soups. But once I did that, started eating meat, chose Papa's side, there'd be no redemption. Amma would never, ever see me the same. That I could treat another one's child like that was the most disgusting thing she could think of. The biggest disrespect to every mother there ever was.

Papa kept trying. He'd planned it. He never told Amma but I'm certain it filled him with glee. My guard was down. They had given me something, a small little pill to calm my nerves before the procedures began. They encouraged me to eat so that I wouldn't get nauseated, a common side effect of the med when taken on an empty stomach. Smart plan to give it to a teenage anorexic.

"Beti, I want you to know I picked this place out special for you. I asked Ashok Uncle, what is THE most veg friendly restaurant close to the clinic? He faxed over their menu right away. I knew you'd want to come because you can finally try."

Despite the pill, I wasn't feeling gratitude for Papa preparing this special outing for us. As Papa was wrapping up his speech about how this was all for me, the waiter approached to fill our glasses and to inform us that our order had been received and was being prepared. Papa saw my face. I was livid. Despite that tiny pill they gave me to prevent an episode like this, Papa knew I was going to scream.

"Beti, I didn't know how you'd be feeling so I ordered many of the vegetarian items, you'll get to try everything, let's eat family style, the appetizers will be here shortly I'm sure." He unwrapped his chopsticks as he spoke. He remembered how to use them, swirling them around his fingers. I had to ask for a fork when the waiter came back.

Watching his hypnotic chopstick formations, it finally dawned on me. We had been seated at a circular table that could seat ten. The glass tabletop spun, that way all members of the party could try a bite of everything. And instead of sitting next to me or across from me, Papa had chosen to sit three chairs down from me. The perfect spot to avoid eye contact. The perfect distance to just be out of range of hearing me speak. I'd have to raise my voice. Embarrass myself. Embarrass him.

"Beti, don't be upset. Just enjoy this meal, you know your whole trip is costing us money. Raj is missing out with his time with his friends to work for me, he is just a kid."

"Raj is older than me."

"Beti, you know how boys are." Papa ended the discussion.

My stomach was starting to boil. I didn't know how I was supposed to eat.

"Papa, I don't know why I couldn't at least look at the menu."

"Beti, you know this talk isn't healthy for you, just sit and eat."

The waiter brought out the appetizers, refilled our drinks, and nodded once we let him know we didn't need anything else besides my fork for now.

After he handed it to me, I used it to cut into my dumpling. And saw it was filled with meat. I don't know what he was thinking. I always examined my food.

"What is this?"

"Beti, don't worry. It isn't meat."

The waiter stopped by to ask if everything was ok so far.

"What are these dumplings stuffed with?" I asked, very kindly so Papa wouldn't get upset.

"Oh, ginger, shiitake mushrooms, onions, and a few other things."

I thanked the waiter and now saw Papa was getting upset. He thought I was trying to get out of eating so I didn't say anything. I worked my magic. Brought a fork to my mouth with a few pieces of the dumpling that didn't look like meat and shoved the rest of the food around my plate.

When the waiter came to take away our small plates, he asked if there was anything wrong with my dumplings. He had seen how many were left and how it looked like I hadn't eaten much of the one I tried. Papa had turned to stare. Daggers.

"Oh, it's just that I don't like mushrooms much. The bites I did have were delicious."

Satisfied with my answer, the waiter let us know the main plates were coming up soon.

"Swati, do not embarrass me here. Just eat what is on your plate and do not cause a scene."

And so, we sat. I wonder how we must have looked to the other diners. Father daughter outing. Seated together but not really.

The waiter arrived with several dishes and expertly slid the glass tabletop as he set the dishes down. There was an art to it, placing the dishes as the table spun. I clapped. Not for Papa but for him. I'm a waitress, I know what's impressive.

Papa let me know he'd make me a plate so that I would try everything.

I thought it was the last straw. The little pill had had no effect on me.

"Papa, how would it feel to you if you were allowed to have a final meal before being placed under watch? A final meal before a series of painful treatments. Where you'd be drugged. And fed through an IV? Do you think maybe you'd want to pick out what you ate?"

"You have always been like your mother." He replied, completely focused on making my plate. "No one else can know what is happening. Only you. No one else can have feelings about what is happening. Only you." He put my plate on the glass and kept the spin of the table as he made his own plate and continued, "You two need to control everything so much you can't even let someone show you an act of love. Feeding you."

Once his plate was in front of him, he asked if I had any questions or wanted to know any of the names of the dishes. He knew I'd be silent. He just wanted to keep talking. I stuck to nibbling on the white rice and green beans on my plate until I heard him say 'mock duck'. I froze, my fork in mid-air.

That had upset him. I was in trouble.

"Beti, I expect you to take a bite out of everything on your plate. I will count. Five dishes, with the rice, at least six bites. Then you can stop, ok?"

I had no choice.

He listed the dishes aloud. I think he thought we were having fun together. Like watching a kid's educational show, learning about a foreign cuisine as we learned our numbers.

"Ok, you have already had the spicy green beans, but you will like this even more, Szechuan mock duck, I asked for it extra spicy for us, we will see if Chinese food or Indian food is spiciest."

It was too hard. I looked down at it and it looked real. There were even little raised bumps. Like it had been freshly plucked. Just for us. Our big meal in the city. Swati and the City.

"Papa, it looks too real. I can't."

That was the last straw. He stood up, walked over to my side, and hovered over me until I ate it. I had to. People had started to stare.

He sat down slowly and quietly spoke, "I don't know why you and your mother always need to be so difficult. You can't trust that I care about you. I won't trick you to eat meat."

"Papa, you can't force trust."

We both pushed food around our plates for a few more minutes. We in the service industry are pretty good at our jobs. The waiter came and worked his magic in reverse. First spinning the table to pick up all the plates and then returning with a cardboard box full of our leftovers. I saw the bill. One hundred and twenty. And Papa always tipped 25%. That's part of the reason why Amma refused to eat out.

I sat in the back seat on the way back to the clinic. I threw up in Papa's back seat next to the cardboard box full of leftovers. Eating didn't help with the nausea after all. Papa drove up to the front doors. He was furious. He had finished yelling at me that I did this on purpose. That I knew Ashok Uncle's family was big and some would be driving to the restaurant with him. How I always had to make everything so difficult for him. I could never allow him to make a good thing out of a very bad situation. I caused so many bad situations.

I opened the back door and crawled out. I turned back and leaned into the car. And then I screamed, in his face, vomit breath and all, "I FUCKING HATE YOU PAPA." I fell to the sidewalk sobbing. Papa came out the driver's side door. I thought he was coming to pick me up. Help me to the automatic doors. Instead, he walked around me and shut the back door. Then he walked back to the driver's side and took off. Left me covered in vomit, sobbing on the sidewalk. I was someone else's problem now.

Cindy tried to think. She could probably get into the library if the Knights guarding it were as drugged as the runaways she and Jenny had hunted had been. But it was risky. And there was always the chance that they had burned all the books years ago.

They loved bragging about their ignorance. The same men who intentionally ate bad pork survived to burn books. How could she ever raise Jenny in this world?

Chapter Nine

I don't need to eat. First the hair and then the meat. I am trying to convince myself it couldn't have been. After all, I don't know if Padmini is even the one cooking any more. How many worker-wives would Jay have checked out? They need a lot of help cleaning. Maintenance in the greenhouse. Sewing up those little herb pouches, however those work. Drying flowers and leaves. I remember being able to chew a couple of chalky colorful tablets when I had diarrhea. Now you need to trade favors for a satchel of Padmini's tea. Knight's America.

I'm really not in the mood for this. Ten days max. I can go one more day without eating. There hasn't been another note. No fucking indication that ANYONE is coming to get me out. That anyone cares.

I am going to go one more day without eating. I made the decision and was doing ok with my new sleep schedule. My meals came right on time. Fresh water. More tomato juice. And these little deep-fried balls of goodness Amma makes. They are just stuffed with ground lentils and spices, rolled in Amma's besan and deep fried. We called them 'dal to go'. Amma never approved of Papa's Indian-Chinese fusion idea but did pick up on his convenience lunch idea. Never gave him credit of course. He owed her more than she did him. *"He wouldn't have any of this without you or me beti."*

I am hungry. I admit it. I used to use affirmations to go without. 'I am not hungry.' 'I can eat tomorrow.' Well, I am fucking ravenous. It's so fucking hard. I think I'm losing my mind.

Right away I wanted to devour them. I took my bites into the doughy portions very slowly. Teeny bites. I wanted to make sure I could peek inside. And I knew right away it wasn't Amma's. Not enough salt. There was still enough light so I ripped it open and pushed my index finger into its center. It wasn't lentils. And it felt what I imagined meat would feel like. What the one bite of 'mock' duck felt like on my tongue. It was disgusting when I tried to chew it. When I chewed. And swallowed.

At least this I could flush. In a few days. I'm hoping it won't be an issue, cause any clogs. Tomorrow is day ten. I think I've been counting right. I suppose it's possible that I fell asleep a bit less than I thought. Or earlier. Which would it be?

I am right. I've gotten the right number of meals. I've been up for all of them. I have not woken up and missed my flush. It really doesn't take long before this shit fucking starts to smell. Pun intended.

Padmini is fucking with my food. I do believe the vitamins are really vitamins. They're good enough for a few more days. I pee neon yellow. Even with as dark as it is in here, I can see that. And fucking smell it too.

I'll be fine. I have that little bag of trail mix (330 calories). I can ration that for a few more days. More than 150 calories for the next two days. And maybe they just open the big door next time. Amma told me I'd get a note. They'd have to let me know. They only receive a little notice of when the exporters are coming. But they come often enough. At least every two weeks. More often than that. That way everyone has what they need. It's a delicate system that falls apart easily, just one borderlands clan could make it so that I'm stuck in here for two more weeks.

Amma always complained about them. She worried. It was a two-day trip there and back. They could stay overnight here but never did. Amma didn't like that. It would have been good for her status, justify the need for more security, have those men stay at the motel. Sure, they'd bring trouble, complications. The Knights always had fun when they were out of their own towns. They could let loose a little more, try something new, something they didn't want to be known for in their own town. It was no disrespect to their Queens if they were lucky enough to have them. The worker-wives don't speak to their Queens about matters like that. But Queens notice if their worker-wives flinch when their Knight passes by. Or if they stop talking to their Queen altogether. Or if their favorite worker-wife just disappears. In another town, it's not their problem. It doesn't impact them quite as much.

They brought a lot of men with them. Two trucks. One for the greenhouse goods. Padmini's salves, tinctures, teas, herbal pouches and poultices. Unbelievably valuable goods. Padmini really knew her stuff. In a time when science wasn't real and women couldn't hold power, she managed to thrive. She ran a whole industry. Her goods were incredibly treasured, and many men protected them on their way back to the Capital City. A two-day drive, no stops, the Knights taking turns driving, sleeping, and keeping watch. Their vehicles seemed like the Wild West. Men on lookout the entire way. More men on lookout to kill them. Lots of men on the lookout to kill anyone who tried to take their treasures. How long has it been this way?

And it was me they chose to test this escape. I'm the very first one! Part of Amma's selling point - no one has ever slept on this mattress. She bought it herself. It was a motel purchase and then funneled here somehow, by Jay, I'm sure.

Those are the types of details that matter to Amma. I'm locked in a room, trying to escape this madness. If I manage to make it out of this will I be raped and killed in the truck on the way to the City? Or when my handler does? I wonder which kind and handsome Knight he could be? The chances of me surviving are close to zero.

I'll never tell Amma that this bed wasn't clean. I know those grunts I hear after my deliveries. They're disgusting. I've had them on me. The hot breath. And I didn't have to see anything to know he made sure to enjoy the bed. Was it Padmini or one of the worker-wives? Amma wouldn't have been crazy enough to demand that detail. How clean everything had to be for me. But I know when I lay my head down that I can smell his stain around me. He's trapped me in it.

So, I keep waiting for the note. No delivery tonight. But I have hopes for the window. I slept during the day. I didn't notice anything different in the worker-wives' patterns. No extra trips up and down the steps. No extra worker-wives packing up all the goods. They'd need to do that before the export Knights arrived. Usually the worker-wives pack while Jay's crew of Knights stand watch. Trust no worker-wives.

If I get a note tonight, that means it will be tomorrow. And if not, repeat. Nothing has really changed, has it? I just have to wait until tomorrow. I'll be trapped on a truck soon enough.

I can wait two days. 330 calories for two days. I have my vitamins. If I get really hungry, I can eat just the dough. I can make the decision to flush them right up until they open that window. Scrape away all the meat. I will have to touch it, but I already have. A few more hours and I'll be out. A new affirmation for me. "A few more hours and I'll be out."

How do I get into the truck? Amma couldn't say. She said to trust them. She didn't trust me to just do what they say. Like I would have any choice. Padmini and Jay wouldn't try to hurt me but no risk and no reward. Think of Abha. What would become of her. It's so selfish of me to not even try. Did I not see Amma? She left her whole family to come here. Traveled across the world. Lost everything and everyone so that her family could have better and I would just let it die here. I wasn't doing anything but dying anyway. What could I possibly do with my life? I'm the same now as I was at 15. More stretch marks. Slightly more self-awareness. Everything else is the same.

What would you say if I get the note and they tell me I'm getting nailed into another room? A tiny crate? That's what I think is going to happen. Do you think they're going to put me in a linen sack and lower me down on a cord? Not to mention these men are rapists. Every fucking single one of them. Amma traveled to this country and risked this a little. Strange men everywhere you go. Papa was here to protect her. She was probably safer here than at home. I know she told me Nana wouldn't let her sisters even talk to another boy. Ever. The assumption was boys will be boys so don't give them temptation. And she is wishing that for me as she wishes it away for Abha. What future did she imagine for us?

Amma was never even alone with a boy until Papa on their wedding night. And she's giving me away to them with no protection. Just my multi-tools and my menstrual cup.

I have a fantasy that I do get caught. I don't know who by. It could be one of the Knights who loads me on to that truck. It could be my handler Knight who receives me in the Capital City. Maybe it's the Knight who helps me on his shoulders so I can hop the wall to freedom. I hate that at the end of every single one of my fantasies, I kiss my Knight. I never kill him.

Cindy had to decide. They could keep moving north and run the risk of running into Knights traveling their trade routes or move further east to find a few textbooks for Jenny. She hadn't been near that town in nearly two years, she'd barely been able to outrun a sniper that had set up on the town hall. A simple food run went bad quickly, she had never been more scared than that night she thought she wouldn't make it back to Jenny. Jenny would have gone looking for her and then those men, those Knights….

A lot could happen in two years, the town could have been taken over by a borderlands clan or be completely burnt to the ground.

She looked over to Jenny, practicing her cartwheels, no clue what was on her momma's mind. Just wanting to play like Cindy had at her age. Cindy had decided they had to try the town again, what point was there to her daughter surviving if all she ever knew was to run and kill?

There had to be at least one book left in that town.

Chapter Ten

They told me 10 days max. Why would they do this to me? It's cruel. A fitting punishment for me. I'll think like Amma. When I was bad, she hit me. After I was done with the crying, done with the shame, she'd ask, "Beti, I didn't want to do that. But what would you have done if you were me?"

Now that I'm her age, older than she was in fact, I can say with great confidence, I would not have beaten the shit out of a small child. Amma takes spiders out, carries them out of rooms, safely, cupped in her hands. Amma says goodbye to them. "Goodbye sweet spider, do your good work outside of my house." It used to embarrass Papa, she'd do it in front of customers. "It is our duty to value every life," she used to say. Now, she looks the other way. She still performs her kindness to all beings. Humans, women specifically, not so much.

Whose life do we value? No one's really. Otherwise, women wouldn't have to trade sex for food with men to feed their children who wouldn't exist without men. I suppose we value the lives of men. Why is that? And why are we so afraid to admit whose lives we value? Would that change things?

After Padmini let me know her disappointment in my poor outfit rotations, I started limiting wearing my skirt over to Padmini's to once a week. Fridays. She'd shamed me effectively; she wasn't a mean girl. She felt guilty and would have me over to bonfire with Jay. Sometimes Jay would have friends over. They'd try to get with me. It was the first time I'd had that type of attention since Mark. Do you think his wife knows he was a baby daddy before her? Did Mark tell her he got a student pregnant before he proposed? Before she said, "I do." Before she gave birth? Did he ever tell her?

Why would he?

Jay's friends would try hard. He and Padmini were always sure to get me alone with whichever of his friends were over. His friends would never stay as long as me. They were just stopping by to pick up from their dealer. Padmini was a star student at university, Jay helped her with the business side of things. Marketing and such.

Padmini bought this farm and had a small operation. It was mainly the apothecary storefront. It always smelled so good. However she made her concoctions, you couldn't help but comment when you stepped in the doors. There was a smaller greenhouse, even further back on the property. Jay had the connections and Padmini had the skills. If Amma had known she would have clapped her hands in delight and blessed them as a perfect match.

But how would Amma ever know? All she saw was a loser who did nothing while Padmini did everything. She didn't know that Padmini got free exposure from his C list connections. I mean of course, I didn't care, they were extremely cosmopolitan to me. Someone who had only been on field trips. Someone whose parents wouldn't let her do anything.

So Padmini's salves and tinctures got exposure. She was able to buy more and more land. Eventually everything had to be under Jay's name, but she was making a lot of money at such a young age. Jay hired some friends to make shipments and other stores out west started carrying her line of goods. And products that were sold after hours. Any money Jay made off the drugs went right back into the business. I am trying to think of how Jay did make the drugs. Padmini did all the work. Jay used his people skills. They weren't impressive, he wasn't all that charismatic. He just happened to know people. You wanted to be one of those people. Padmini wouldn't have been so successful without him.

I don't think she ever thanked him. I'm sure he never thanked her either, but it was different from Amma and Papa. Not an expectation of thanks but a waiting for gratitude. Padmini wouldn't be anywhere without Jay and Jay wouldn't be anywhere without Padmini. Amma and Papa accepted they were a team. Padmini and Jay didn't think that way.

Whichever of his friends he left me with, it didn't matter because I'd only be thinking of him. It's been years and I still don't know what happened. He wasn't mysterious, he didn't really pay attention to me, and yet all I wanted was more time with him. He was famous.

Mark pursued me. Jay ignored me.

It's so funny though. You wouldn't have recognized him. Unless you were raised by TV like I was. His show had only been on for a season, back in the early 90s. He was probably 12 or so at the time. He played Patrick on the very terrible and rightfully canceled family sit-com *10 Items or Less*. It aired on Friday nights and was about Patrick's family. He had taken on the responsibility of his eight younger siblings while his Mom worked (very romantic) nights at the grocery store. Her husband had just died. The show was ripped apart by everyone. What family values were those? Leaving her 12-year-old son to raise her other children. Viewers were supposed to double over in laughter at her pain as she epilated her legs, she needed to look sexy, maybe let that married supermarket manager feel her smooth legs in order to get that raise. It was fucked up. And still better than where we are at today.

He'd get so mad if you ever called him Patrick. A silent mad though. I saw it once. Padmini and I were making grilled cheese sandwiches for everyone around the bonfire. One of Jay's customers had stopped by to make a purchase and brought friends with him. Long Hair and No Hair let's call them. That was a no-no to begin with. Jay was incredibly careful about who he let on the property. It didn't matter to him that Padmini only had one friend. She was only allowed one visitor, he trusted that I wouldn't talk. Padmini had convinced him. I don't know how hard she had to try.

The mood around the campfire instantly changed when there were two extra visitors. There were always plenty of seats but Jay didn't invite customers to sit with us. They could stop by, purchase, and leave. He didn't want people sticking around to use the bathroom, scope out the farm, figure out how to steal from him. Long Hair had an over familiarity with Jay. Sat down with us at the bonfire and grabbed a stick to poke the fire with. Maybe he was nervous. It didn't matter because it was too late. I could see Jay's clenched jaw. I noticed everything about him. Jay's younger friend Adam suggested they get moving along and the customer was well aware of the warning he was getting, there were clear rules for this transaction - don't bring strangers. But it was too late. No Hair must not have understood Adam's warning. He asked what the big deal was and his question was immediately followed by Long Hair asking Jay if anyone had told him he looked like Patrick from that one TV show. Jay shut his eyes and Padmini told me we should go inside. I resisted; I was trying to get one of the grilled cheeses out of the pudgie pie pan. I was so worried about not being around Jay while also making sure that I wasn't burning myself making his sandwich that I didn't understand why I was smelling burning hair. Why was there screaming?

Adam had given no warning. He had been fiddling with a stick while he stood. At some point he had set it on fire and then stood beside Long Hair.

"Oh no," Adam said, in a completely flat tone, "Stop, drop, and roll on your way out."

Jay got up and went into the house and Padmini followed. It was just Adam and me. The visitors had put Long Hair's fire out and were running to their car.

"I'm sorry you had to see that," Adam said to me, "I'm even more sorry we had to lose a big customer. That's just the way it is sometimes. When you see someone's true colors, it's best to meet them where they're at."

"You sound like my mom," I said. This was the first time Adam had ever spoken to me. He was cute but too young for me. He'd been hanging around Jay and Padmini's place longer than me though.

"Your mom must be a smart lady," he smiled at me, "May I please have a grilled cheese?"

Maybe that's why Jay let me hang around so much. I could keep Padmini and Adam company. I followed the rules. I respected the way Jay did things. That summer I watched. With everyone else Jay would just jet. I'd watch, he wouldn't even say goodbye, he'd just get up and leave until his friends felt uncomfortable enough being left alone with Adam or until Padmini came out and told them to leave because she had a business to run. I was welcome to stick around as long as I wanted. I did help Padmini out and also, she felt really sorry for me. She knew what my parents were like. Even if they seemed better than her parents. I didn't have anywhere else to go.

So I'd stick around the house and eventually Jay would make his way back to me. Well probably not to me. Back to wherever Padmini had set me up for the afternoon, doing tasks you'd give a kindergartner. Jay would sit with me or he'd at least send Adam to me, have him tell me hello. At those Friday night bonfires, the boys he left me with were always so forward. I wore those skirts for Jay, but they took advantage. Placing their hand on my bare thigh, "*I thought you might want to warm up*", or massaging my shoulders, "*your body must be tired from helping Padmini all day*".

Adam would just watch. And I'd always get up and walk inside the house. Adam never followed. Sometimes Padmini and Jay would be arguing over some bullshit and sometimes I'd walk in to catch Padmini getting mad at Jay for grabbing her ass. On occasion the friend they were trying to set me up with wouldn't even try. He'd ignore me or try to buddy up to Adam. Padmini and Jay would always come out together. When they'd had enough.

"I can ask him to stop you know," Padmini said probably halfway through that summer.

"What do you mean?" I asked, probably drying off a dish or doing something else to help because I feel worthless unless I'm not helping someone helping me.

"If you don't want to get set up with any of Jay's friends."

I didn't have much to say to that. She didn't know about Tulika. She didn't know me.

"Well, how about Adam? He's cute, isn't he?" Padmini tried to press.

"He looks 12 Padmini."

"He's actually exactly your age Swati."

"You know that's not how this works Padmini. I have to wait."

Padmini knew I wasn't an angel but she knew how Indian parents can be.

"Swati, have some fun with Adam. If you want something more, most of these guys have money. That's all dads care about. That their daughter will be taken care of."

"Is that why you're with me?" Neither of us had noticed Jay had entered the kitchen.

"What the fuck do you think Jay? Are we living like we have money?"

"Because you need to expand and expand and expand Padmini!"

I tried to become small. I wanted to leave but I didn't want to draw attention to myself. So, I stayed. Until they both stormed out. They didn't give a shit about me. I was too young to understand. I thought everything should be about me always. So, I finished whatever task I had been working on. I heard Padmini crying after she took a shower, or at least ran one. I saw Jay on my way out. Had he been waiting for me on the steps?

"I'll walk you."

I hadn't worn my skirt that day but did change into some platform sandals as I had neared the top of the driveway. I wasn't sure how I'd get out of this one.

"It's ok Jay."

"I could use the air Swati."

"It's like, a really long walk. Almost five miles, that'll be ten for you."

"I can make my way home Swati. I'll call Adam to pick me up. Or I'll stay over with you."

I couldn't help but jerk my head to look at him. He was smiling. He never, ever smiled. He looked great when he smiled. It's like his eyes were shining. I didn't need to say anything, what could I possibly say? So, I smiled back.

We walked down the driveway in silence until he eventually stopped. I quickly noticed and halted as well. He stared at me expectantly.

"What's going on?" I asked.

"Are you going to walk home in those?"

"What do you mean?"

"You said it yourself Swats, it's almost five miles."

Had he just called me Swats?

"I'll be ok," I said and turned, my ankle slightly buckling over my heel before I caught myself and started walking.

"Your feet are going to be bleeding."

"I'll be fine!" I called back to him, "I do this every day!" As I'm writing this, I realized I called back to him flirting. I was hoping he'd chase after me, sweep me up, carry me down the driveway. I've watched too much TV.

"I KNOW." He yelled back.

I stopped and turned around. He could catch up or he could turn around. We were at a standstill. I'd count to 30. I tried to influence him however I could, *let me be alone with you, I'll do anything to be alone with you.* And at 30, I turned around and started walking. I held it together for a few steps and then heard his steps catching up behind me. I had willed him to come to me.

"I can see you, you know," he said. Reaching behind me to snap off a twig, catching me by the waist when he threw me off balance.

"Follow me!" he said, jogging slightly into the woods, "You'll wanna change your shoes though!" He had turned around, jogging backwards, I could see his charismatic smile. His blue eyes were twinkling. Had my boring brown eyes ever done that? For anyone?

I stood there for a few moments. And looking back, I'm surprised I didn't just keep walking down the driveway. That is absolutely what I'd predict me doing. But Jay's smile had pulled me. And I wanted to make him smile more. So, I reached into my bag and swapped my shoes. I absolutely would have twisted my ankle if I had denied it.

I didn't run after him though. I tried to be sexy. I thought I sauntered over. I'm sure it's just that I walked slowly. I really just didn't want to fall face first into mud. He never went too far ahead, he waited for me, leaning against a tree.

"What is this all about?" I asked.

He stood there, smiling. Not answering. I started getting scared.

"Jay?" I was trying to shake something out of him, "Well, fine then, I'm going." Before I could even turn, he grabbed me by the waist, pulling me into his warmth. I could feel his sweat on my back, his breath on my neck.

"Look up," he said one hand pointing over our heads, the other slipping under my t-shirt, "If you wouldn't mind, I'd love to see your smile. Save it on camera." And so I looked up and smiled for the camera.

Cindy had to make a decision, to leave Jenny like she did the last time she went to this town or to take advantage of her help. Jenny's motor skills had improved so much in two years. She was a more accurate fighter than Cindy now. But she hadn't had the time to develop the ability to see the tactical advantages like her momma had, that Cindy had been trained to sense since she was 17. This moment felt like fate to Cindy, like everything she had experienced had all been training specifically for this. Her whole life. Since her own momma had put her in charge.

What would Jenny have wanted? If she could have had a normal childhood? She'd love to read, do puzzles, she'd probably love music, love to dance.

Cindy realized it didn't matter what Jenny wanted. What mattered was Jenny's reality. She'd never be able to do any of those things in peace if Cindy was dead. Cindy had so much to teach her.

Jenny could at least help her stake out the town. That would be safe. Safer.

Chapter Eleven

There's good news and bad news. Good news first. Always. We can handle bad news when we know there's good news. Really good news: I'm getting out. Tomorrow. I got a special delivery this morning. A note, just one word written in Amma's Devanagari: kal. She knew I tried to learn on my own. If anyone had found it, they would have had to ask Amma or Raj to translate. If it went to Raj, he would have denied being able to read *("We only speak Knight's American here")* and said he could try to ask Amma. Amma would make something up if she was interviewed. She has built up a lot of trust with Sheriff Paulson. Besides, they don't know what they don't know, and they honestly don't care enough to learn.

Tomorrow.

So, I had to. I celebrated. I will never be able to thank Amma enough. I'm scared and excited for freedom. I've been starving. I was so hungry and I was so happy. It was a real special delivery. A samosa AND chai. And fresh, cold, water. My head has been hurting so bad and I'm so thirsty all the time. My spit is always so thick in my mouth. I can forget about rationing now. I had saved enough water for one more day. I gulped the freshly delivered water, I waited a bit for my spit to thin in my mouth, it always gets so thick when I'm waiting to eat, and when it did, I wanted to savor the chai. The samosa was Amma's. Everything was still warm. I cried just holding the food. It was safe.

Now the bad news. While I was waiting to drink my tea, savoring the scent, I tried to tune out Jay's rhythmic grunting. It was disgusting and I had to be silent. If I could hear them, they could hear me. He's been having trouble doing his Knightly duty, does Padmini know I can hear? I hear what he's asking her to do so he can get hard. It was so long ago that it wasn't like that for us, we are all older now. I didn't want to hear, I don't want Padmini to know so I focused on my chai and willed myself not to hear Jay fucking Padmini in the middle of the night, turned on by his delivery to me. After he was done, I sat in the silence, only wanting to enjoy the chai made with Amma's hands but remembering when Jay was done how he'd just lay on me, I wanted to throw him off but didn't want to be rude. With Mark, it was over so quick, he'd always have to leave right away. Couldn't risk anyone finding out. Thinking about all of this in the silence, I began to hear someone's whispers through the vents.

"Amma."

"Amma, can you hear me."

"Amma, please, I don't have much time."

Hearing Jay's fucking noises through the vents didn't scare me, it disturbed me. Hearing this was absolutely terrifying. I didn't know what to do. Amma was here? Was Padmini holding her here with me?

"*I'm trying to help you."* A desperate whisper came through the vent.

I don't know what came over me. I heard fear in her voice.

"Who's there?" I stood up and tilted my head up to the vent and whispered as quietly as I could. Hoping to myself that I was doing the right thing.

"Amma? Is that you?" Her voice returned to me through the vent.

"No. Who are you? Do you know why Amma would be here?" I was getting frantic. How could it be? Is that how I had gotten Jay's special delivery?

"My Nani told me my Amma would be here," my heart dropped into my gut when she said this, "You can call me Tulie. It's short for Tulika."

There's no way I can explain to you my reaction, I was silently crying while silently laughing. Hugging myself. Tulika at Padmini's? Was she a worker-wife for Jay? Why would she be here in the middle of the night? Was any of this real?

"I don't have much time. I can pass my message along to you, whoever you are." She again spoke to me.

I stood on my tiptoes and whispered to her, trying my hardest to be both quiet and strong, "It is me. I'm your Amma." Tears fell down my face. I was feeling my spit get thick again in my mouth from all the tears.

"Oh Amma! We don't have much time, but we will later. Nani says to be on your guard. You can't trust anyone but just trust her. We have a plan. You'll be fine, don't attack anyone."

"Tulie, how are you here? Are you saying there's a change in our plan?" How old would she be today? Does she look like me? Does she look like Amma?

"Amma, we don't have time. Just stay alert. I love you Amma. I must go."

"Tulie!" I called out to her in a whisper, all while knowing she had to have gone. I didn't think to say I love you back.

My mind turned to the worst of places while I sipped Amma's chai.

Had Tulie been the one making my deliveries?

Had Tulie been the one under Jay as he grunted?

Had Tulie been hidden from me by Amma?

Where had she been?

Why was she kept from me?

Who would I be today if we hadn't been torn apart?

And still, knowing Amma had kept us apart, our biological ties wouldn't let her. Tulika came to help me.

So, the good news had some very bad news attached to it. I'm trying to stay brave. I'm not sure how I'll be able to sleep. If I should. I will be packing you, well this journal, up for a bit.

I can't escape now, knowing she's here. I'll die rather than risk losing her again.

But Abha. It's too late for me, but not too late for her. All of this is for her.

But what about Tulie? My daughter matters too. What can come of her life? Maybe Amma would let her go in my place. What was Amma thinking with this plan? Is it too late?

Amma was trying to help. She would be so mad to know I spoke back into the vent. But if I hadn't...If I did what I WANTED to do, what my body told me to do, shrink back, pretend not to exist, just take it, then I never would have learned she's still here. Because I left the comfort I've found by hiding, I have found my daughter. My daughter fucking found ME.

"Don't attack anyone."

What is waiting for me on the other side of that door?

There's a change in plans waiting for me. I can't quite recall, did Amma tell Tulika to give me the message or did Tulika overhear Amma making her plans? Amma always looks for an opportunity.

And where was Padmini?

Padmini has risen to power, that much is true. It's possible she's too busy to dabble into this type of grunt work. When she's not doing her ceremonies at Gallows Park, she's got a lot of responsibility under Knight. Her proximity to him makes her a local celebrity, probably why her and Jay make such a strong power couple for him. You can gather to watch her remove the stitches too, she does it so quickly, no popcorn or lavender tea on those days but the young lads love to watch and follow the poor Knight home, bully him to the core of his self-worth the way only a pack of teenage boys can. Women get to enjoy The Sewing twice, first the catharsis of watching a man who insulted a Queen's honor have his lips sewn shut by a woman. Then again over the following weeks when the young men she knows report back to her how they threw rocks and rotten vegetables his way, herding him out of town. Young pups nipping him in the ankle, so he'll get back in line. Once you've got the scars on your lips, you can live out in the borderlands or you can snivel your way back up the

Knight's order. Some choose to but you never make your way back up that pecking order. No Knight would ever allow you near their Queen. Worker-wives are allowed to refuse you. It's rare and the Knights try to intimidate them out of it, but they must respect their decision.

The women are the backbone of it all. Knight's most precious currency.

There's the hard labor cleaning up mold and waste or putting out rolling fires, all away from your family and friends, and the people you know. And there's also the hard labor of farming, town maintenance like shoveling the snow, mowing the properties, picking up the waste generated by your former friends and family (don't try calling them neighbors, they live in freedom, you live in jails; those men are Knights, you men are footmen). Can't you just save up for a trip to the canteen since no worker-wife here would ever lay beneath you? Can you *really* survive in the borderlands? Killing people for food? Amma and I overheard stories at The Chai House. Knights saying there wasn't much chance for them to overtake their vehicles to steal nutrition boxes so the outsiders had been killing each other, roasting their limbs at night.

It's always better to stay with the familiar. It's hard labor and you're segregated from anyone and anything you used to like but you get three squares. Fresh water. You aren't sleeping in the elements. You have a bed. Do you think the other dissidents get that? What would you expect to happen after disrespecting a Queen? It is the only crime you get a second chance from.

Do you think they've found out Padmini isn't Jay's Queen? It all stemmed from that first day in the woods between us.

"Is that why you're with me?"

Padmini wanted to get married. She loved Jay. But she never brought it up again. If Jay loved her, he'd ask on his own. And he never did. Amma's warning came true, he was able to get the milk for free. And there was no reason for Padmini to complain, she was able to graze the greenest of pastures because of it.

It was close to dusk. Cindy and Jenny would do a loose perimeter check now and again throughout the day tomorrow if it seemed safe. Cindy knew where the library was, it was a matter of getting there safely. Figuring out, who, if anyone, was left in this little town. If anyone would be staked out at the shopping center where the library was. Even if they made it there safely, the books could have been burnt in the riots or to keep a family warm at night. Who the fuck knows what could be left, she just had to hope there was something useful, something valuable for Jenny to learn.

Cindy's momma hadn't exactly cared about Cindy's education and Cindy went to school hungry most days so she didn't care about it either when it was left up to her. She was seen as a troublemaker instead of someone with troubles. But there wasn't time to feel sorry for herself. This was about Jenny now. How she could provide a better future for her. At least try to provide some future.

She went to check on her daughter and saw Jenny was staring at something, with her mouth wide open. Cindy scooted next to her and physically shut Jenny's jaw gently with her index and middle fingers.

"Don't make faces like that or you'll get stuck that way," Cindy joked. Jenny had no reaction though. Cindy went to follow Jenny's gaze and understood why Jenny seemed to be in shock.

There were four kids walking around. Not doing much but not afraid to be walking together, out in the open. Cindy didn't want to risk everything to help them. She had just come to this cursed town for a book. Any book. And now this.

'Am I any better than my own momma?' Cindy asked herself.

Chapter Twelve

I don't have much to pack. Just you and this pen. I have my backpack ready to go. It won't take much time to put you away. Amma reinforced over and over, when it happened I would have to move quickly. She didn't know though. I will hear them working on the pegboard when it's time to leave. Time for me not to attack.

I need to find out from Amma. Is Tulie real? Has she been hiding my daughter from me?

She came again last night. And again, this morning.

They arranged so there'd be no worker-wives today. I haven't heard any steps. No low voices. It must be happening today. It has to happen today. I can't stay in here anymore. I'm losing it.

I stood under the vent. I don't know for how long. Listening so hard. It was worth it. She came and spoke to me, in whispers, "Amma, I hope you're listening, I must be quick. Whatever happens today, I love you. We are going to be together soon. Trust yourself Amma. I love you Amma."

"I love you Tulika," I whispered back. I don't know if she stood on the other end silently crying, the same as me. I hope I find out. What has Amma been keeping from me? A change in plans can mean anything. I can hear their voices now. They're coming here to get me. To move me to freedom. I don't know if Padmini will be on the other side. Do I hug her? Avert my eyes? Touch her feet?

Cindy had Jenny stay put to keep an eye on the children so that Cindy could follow them. Jenny had her bird calls down pretty well. Cindy didn't know where Jenny picked it up from, she couldn't even whistle. It didn't matter though; Cindy wouldn't stray too far. Jenny could signal her if necessary. Cindy wasn't planning on getting into any trouble.

Cindy maneuvered through the terrain and was able to get to a higher spot for a bird's eye view. It worked out well, she could keep an eye on Jenny while also watching the kids on her binoculars. The way she obtained things made it hard for her to explain stealing to her daughter.

As the children walked she realized they were four boys. They didn't play in any way. They walked a little lethargically, she was sure they must be hungry too. She'd imagine four boys walking just a few years ago, they'd be causing a ruckus, throwing things, knocking into one another. She could tell one was the leader, not only was he the biggest, but he was also the loudest. He was shouting directions at the others, nothing seemed helpful, just telling them what they were already doing.

Cindy watched as they made their way to a playground. She spent a lot of her time with regrets and she was adding another to the list. If only she had been a little less focused on watching the children behave. Seeing if they were still kids or not. If she had instead done a more thorough environmental scan, she would have noticed the playground earlier. Seen the lanky girl tied with her arms behind her back to the cold metal of the swing set. Saw the gag in her mouth. Noticed the blossoming of her belly. That she was barely dressed.

Then maybe she could have saved her.

PART TWO

Chapter One

It's been a while, hasn't it? I lost time in the closet. They had me in there for over two weeks. How much weight did I lose? "Do I look skinny Amma?" She didn't say. Somehow, I lost track of time. My Gamer Girl is still flashing 11:11. Nobody checked my backpack. Nobody checked the room. Nobody checked me.

I was ushered out of my closet. It reminded me of those tabloids I would read in waiting rooms or waiting in line to check out at the grocery store with Amma. Before the Knights. Jay was even on the cover once. I didn't know him at the time, it was over his emancipation. The ones I liked had celebrities pretending to cover their heads with their security guard's jackets as they ran to their cars, trying to outrun the paparazzi. How many of them got access to bunkers? Did their private security protect them?

At the time all of us knew those celebrities had paid a lot of money to arrange for the paparazzi to be there. Jay had gotten offers like that; some celebs didn't care. At least they were being talked about.

"Look how fat Kelly is now."

"Can you believe Andreah's plastic surgery?"

"Chanel's purposeful but made to look not that way's nipple slip. Didn't she know how desperate she seemed?"

Papa would let me read them. If Amma had driven me, she would judge so I'd select *The Weekly Digest* instead, catch up on real news, use Amma's wasted time to make something of myself. Those tabloids were so good though. Did you enjoy them? Wishing you could afford their clothes, even if they were ugly and you'd have nowhere to wear them. Being able to judge from up high on my throne, I didn't need to show my nipples for attention, she really was desperate, pathetic.

Except I had done that for Jay. Let him record me. And us. I'd visit Padmini and hope it'd be one of the days he'd be in a better mood. Want to walk me back home. I made excuses, told myself that Padmini was used to him wandering off. He had business to do. I'd seen him do it to her all summer. I couldn't judge their relationship; I'd only ever been exposed to Amma and Papa. Mark had only wanted one thing. I had never even been in a relationship.

There had been a big change in plans. When they opened the door, the light in the basement overpowered my eyes. I couldn't believe what I was seeing. It was Amma's tiny frame, wearing her grey Senior Queen head covering around her neck like a dupatta. As my eyes adjusted I saw she was covering her nose and mouth with one end of the dupatta, avoiding my stink, I suppose. Jay was there with another Knight. He looked familiar to me, I later remembered him as Adam. I hadn't seen him in years. The only one of Jay's friends who never tried to get with me when we were left alone together at those Friday campfires.

Amma removed her hand from her mouth, dropping her dupatta and used her index finger to shush me. Her nails were painted red. She hadn't painted her nails in forever. Said it was a waste with how much she had to wash her hands.

I startled when Adam reached for me. He held onto me with one arm and Amma kept her finger to her lips while her other hand wrapped her Senior Queen scarf around her head before pointing that index finger at me. Adam covered my head with something. A Senior Queen's disguise for someone who'd never even be a Queen. I was too old for dress up; this was risky if anyone saw.

Jay led the way up the stairs. Adam placed a hand on my shoulder to guide me up the stairs. If Amma hadn't been there would he have steered me at the small of my back? Amma was there and took the rear. Even if I wanted it, it would never happen. I followed everyone's lead and walked quietly. I was still so thirsty. I couldn't wait for a glass of water, but I didn't understand why I was being taken upstairs, why I wasn't being packed away onto a truck.

Adam gently pushed me through the house as Jay led me on his path. Where was Padmini? Was Tulika here? Two flights of stairs and I was seeing stars again. Adam grasped me tighter, helped me come back to the present, supported me so I wouldn't fall. Jay opened the door to his guest bathroom and gestured for me to step inside. I had washed up in here before. I stood still and Adam dropped his guiding hand from my shoulder. Amma stepped up beside me and said, "Chalo beti."

It was glorious. She ran me a hot bath, Padmini must have left some of her bath pouches. I don't remember when Amma's cared for me in this way. She helped comb out my braids. The smell that rose from the bath was so fresh, lavender and eucalyptus. Smelling the steam alone was surreal, just as before I didn't know if I was dreaming. I asked Amma and she pinched me. Hard on my triceps. I can see the fading bruise on my arm. It hadn't been a dream.

But even after that pinch I was so disoriented. I asked Amma about Tulie and she ignored me. I had to be patient. Wait for when she was ready to talk.

Amma helped me take off my robe and held my hand as I stepped into the bath. Averting her eyes at my naked body. The one she had birthed.

When she asked if I needed help bathing, her tone let me know that she didn't want to help. It was ok though. I still asked for help, and she tried for a minute to wash my back, passively rubbing the cloth across my shoulder blades before handing it back to me. We both tried. It didn't go well last time, when I got back from the clinic and she had to help me shower before doing puja. She stepped out of the room so I could towel off and I had fainted. When I came to, she was mad at me, at my lack of independence. For scaring her again. My second day home I was feeling much stronger. I didn't need her help showering so made my way to the bathroom on my own, I didn't need to wait for her. I knew she'd be mad but when I turned on the tub, I saw she had already beat me to it. She had set a stool, bucket, and washcloth in the tub. She had no intention of helping me that day. Why would she?

"Why should I help you beti? No one helped me when I was your age. Did you know I had to raise everyone around me?"

That was who had been waiting for me on the other side of the door.

That was who had volunteered me into that closet, to smuggle me up north, to experiment with Jay and Padmini's power.

Amma kept her eyes on the tile, moving so she could stand with her back to the tub, "Be sure to clean everywhere Swati. You really smell."

"Thanks, Amma. Maybe now that I'm older I've figured out how to wash myself."

"All this is happening, and you are looking to start a fight with me? After I saved your life?"

I didn't say anything. It was always easier to just not say anything with Amma. She was always looking for a problem when it came to me. And I can say with honesty that there are plenty to find.

"There's been a change in plans beti."

"Yes, Amma, I got your message."

"What message? What nonsense is this?"

"Tulika let me know you sent your message. Expect a change of plans and do not attack."

"Accha Swati, beti, I need you to listen to me," Amma started playing with her Senior Queen's scarf. A nervous tic she always had, it came out when she felt on stage, like when we'd host Diwali for the local Indian families, playing with her pallu or dupatta, needing something to adjust because nothing was ever perfect like it needed to be, "Enjoy your bath for now, just listen. No more about Tulika this and that, please. No more questions. When you are done cleaning up, you are going to get a little dressed up. You aren't going to need to sneak away, we will save Abha right here. This is good news, nahi?"

I pulled my head under the water and started counting. I couldn't even get to ten. When I came back up she was still talking, she hadn't even noticed me slip under, "You let me do your hair up to show your neck a little bit. Raj will speak for you and then we will just need to set a date. Hopefully in two weekends, it should be an auspicious date and Sheriff Paulson will really want to show off, the motel will be full and with people who can pay." I couldn't see her face but Amma sounded awfully proud of herself.

"Amma, what did you do?" I asked, suddenly noticing that the bath water was starting to lose its heat.

"Beti, no resistance today, please. I do not want any fights, ok?"

My eyes darted around the bathroom, I couldn't remember bringing you, but Amma must have carried my backpack up the steps to the bathroom. If this journal got misplaced, if Adam had taken it... In my frantic worry my concentration had drifted, realizing Amma was asking me if I understood.

"Amma, what is happening?" I wanted to understand and couldn't.

"Beti, I have found you a very suitable match."

"Amma, who is it?" Who could it possibly be, my stomach felt so sick, I was going to be sick in this tub.

Amma turned around, she looked above my head, still afraid to look at my eyes, at my body. I saw she was smiling. She was incredibly happy. She was feeling very proud.

"Swati, you are a very sweet girl. And still, you can be so simple sometimes. I don't want you to feel bad at all, when I say these things. This is why I know you'll be such a good wife. You are helping our family. Abha will be able to thrive because of your power."

I was starting to shiver, I began to lift myself out of the tub and Amma reached out to me, enveloping me in a warm towel. Combing out my hair. As she helped oil my skin and plait my hair into a side braid (*"show off your neck a little beti")* she explained.

First, she let me know not to worry. Padmini would be ok. She is moving into a role more suited for someone of her class and family. Amma was helping her, she's best off with our help. It will strengthen the whole town.

Knight had reached out to Jay early on when his campaign started picking up steam. Jay had dismissed the fame he got as a childhood star, he'd absolutely end you if you called him Patrick today, I guarantee you that. But he didn't mind the internet fame he got from his broadcast *4&20;* write to Jay for advice and he'd take on 4 of your issues in 20 minutes. All while using what

Padmini was illegally growing. He wanted to use his rejected fame to do something good, legalize it, get drug users out of prison. If people still wanted to get their advice from a nearly middle aged, former child star who admitted he used, that could change the way people thought about drugs and the people who used them.

Knight had some horribly archaic views, about almost everything if you ask me. But he won the popular vote in every single state in part to his empathetic speeches to parents, families, and loved ones.

"Forgive them. Forgive yourself. Of course, you self-medicated. Your purpose was taken from you. Your biological purpose was taken, and we are all hurting because of it. We are all animals after all. And we all know monkeys eat fermented fruit."

So, he won. No more jail time for drug charges. Rehabilitation instead. The Knights will help you select your choice of hard labor. People resisted. People fled. Lots of available jobs doing private security. If you had any sort of experience, you could go into the private military. The Knights started as a militia after all. The future was now.

I made one of those little mistakes again. No more jail time for illegal drug charges. Knight made his fortune off his family's pharmaceutical business. And so he was able to work with Jay and Padmini to patent several types of flowers and more. Lots of flowers have lots of different uses.

Hello foxglove. Thank you for helping me when I feel bloated during my time of the month.

Hello dandelion. Thank you for brightening my day and my salads.

Hello poppy. Thank you for helping me when I am in pain.

When Knight was campaigning, Jay rejected his anti-feminist views on his broadcast. Held debates. But at some point Knight offered him a deal he couldn't refuse and he was able to see the reasons behind why Knight wanted to try to do things the old-fashioned way. His number of listeners grew. People loved to hate him. You disagreed with Jay on a lot but when you agreed with him, you agreed with him. He was a reasonable guy. Referred to Padmini as his Queen on the broadcast. She was the first. They made it on to a few tabloids. Lakshmi Auntie found out and was proud. I couldn't believe it when Amma told me. But I could. *"All they care about is whether they have money."*

Everyone loved Padmini. She was a modest, successful, modern businesswoman. Her entire business existed only to support her husband's work. Women started buying more of her goods. They wanted to be associated with the brand, support a business that supported their values. They wanted to be Pimply Padmini.

I'd stopped coming by long before all this. It was too hard being around Jay. He was never going to leave Padmini and it's not like I really even wanted to be with him. Be his wife. Be his girl. I just wanted him to want me. And Padmini had to know something was up.

I did ask her one time when I was ringing her up why she'd encourage Jay to call her his Queen. How misogynistic it was considering she was the one who ran the business. In front of Amma I lost my temper and swore. She was a female owned business for fucks sake. Padmini had her PR worked out but with me she was honest, "Because it's good for business Swati. We are expanding like never before. I'm going to be able to hire more women because of how much Knight's advertising is helping us. So what if it sets feminism back a tiny bit? It's actually helping the women in this shit state. Jay is working to REDUCE arrests."

And now Amma was telling me that Padmini had hurt a lot of people through her fraudulent misrepresentation. Amma knew they had never been married and was acting like Padmini had lied to us. Letting me know that what her, Jay, and Knight had worked out would be better for Padmini than all other alternatives.

"You've been working with Knight?" I whispered, watching her face in the mirror as she finished my plait.

Amma nodded her head in affirmation, "Yes, this is really good for all of us. I know you are feeling off so please just be quiet and trust. Everything is ok and you know Raj will be here too. Just sit and let us handle it."

I nodded and saw Amma grab a pink scarf from her bag. One of the pink scarves that indicate a girl has her cycle and has passed her Queen qualifications.

"I don't understand Amma." I was feeling queasy. I would have to have been the oldest person to ever wear the pre-Queen scarf. I started laughing. I wanted to vomit into this dupatta.

Amma hushed me, hit me sharply on my spine with the paddle of her hairbrush to shut me up.

"Amma. Who. Is. My. Match. Tell me."

"Swati, don't play dumb. You will be matched with Jay. Everyone is very pleased with the match. Both matches are very, very good."

"Amma, I can't. Padmini."

"Don't worry about Padmini. She's getting her very own color even. No one will ever touch her. Jay wronged her," Amma was pleased with herself.

She opened the door to guide me out and Adam was standing directly outside. What had he heard?

Our eyes met and he started to say something and then stopped. Led me down the stairs. This time no need for touch.

I smelled Amma's cooking. When we got to the kitchen, the table was covered with my favorite dishes. Amma pulled my elbow, telling me no as I attempted to speed up, to race to the table embrace Raj. Maybe she thought I was racing for the food. I couldn't do either I suppose. I wouldn't eat until Raj ate first. Here, I wouldn't eat until Jay had his first bite.

Jay sat at the head of the large wooden table. This was new to me. It was meant for large gatherings. Padmini could have had 14 people over for dinner. Not that we did things like that anymore.

Raj sat to Jay's right. Adam pulled the chair out to Jay's left. I stood until I realized he did that for me. After I sat down, Adam seated himself next to Raj. Amma started to make plates from the dishes on the table.

Jay smiled at me, "We can get right down to business. I'm sure you're hungry. How could you not be? I hope you enjoyed your stay?" He was joking and none of us laughed.

"Amma and I have worked out all the details for our nuptials," he continued, "Raj will sign, then me, and finally, Adam as witness. Then we can get to the real reason we're all here. To enjoy Amma's cooking!"

When did Jay stop calling Amma Deepali Auntie? That's what he always did. The men slid the papers around and Amma began serving the plates. She chose to sit all the way at the other end of the large table from us. I could read it either way, she was trying to show her power was equal to Jay's or she was making herself small, as a Senior Queen should. Let the Knights enjoy the company of a pre-Queen. A younger model.

The men talked. Idle chit chat about the weather, and its impact on potential for trade and more residents at the motel. I didn't push my food around. Amma had made me a smaller plate and I ate everything. No one had to count my bites. Jay insisted we all drink to our union. I swallowed my wine in one gulp and felt it immediately. Raj was concerned and mad, I could tell. Jay loved it. I saw that when Amma saw Jay smiled, she smiled too. She caught me looking and wrinkled her nose at me. Satisfied with her match.

Where was Padmini? I had to wait to ask Amma, Raj hadn't made any effort to speak to me since I had sat down. Simply answering Jay's questions about me, being an actor. I could ask in private but not here. Jay had instructed Amma and I to wait here. Raj was driving us home but Jay was insisting Raj stay, to celebrate for another round in the sitting room. And to try out a new blend of flower he'd be premiering soon. The ladies could wait a bit. "They always need rest," he joked.

Amma and I stood on the stairs while we waited for Raj to bring the car closer. Jay helped me to the car. He hugged me goodbye. He was allowed to now. No one could stop him. As long as he didn't do a few things, he could do a lot more than before. He let me know he was looking forward to our future. He shut the door and we drove away. On the way home, I asked Raj where Abha was, who was watching her and they both pointedly ignored me, Amma turning her head to stare out the window, Raj refusing to meet my eyes in the rear-view mirror. I had upset them already, first night out of the box.

I had so many questions and no one to ask. I wanted to find Tulika. When we arrived back at the motel I said goodnight and thank you to Raj. He didn't acknowledge me, just walked straight towards his place.

Amma walked me to my door and said, "We have two days."

I asked Amma as she turned the key in the lock to my room, "Where are we going in two days?"

She opened the door and waited for me to step inside, "Central Home and Hearth. We need to certify your virginity before we can set the date."

Cindy knew what she had to do. She hesitated to act because she didn't want Jenny to see the cruelty of this world. But that girl couldn't have been much older than Jenny. Jenny had already seen so much cruelty in this world. She had taught her daughter it was their responsibility to stop it.

Cindy packed up her binoculars and placed them in their case, every day it seemed that the Knight's logo faded a little bit more. She couldn't wait until it was erased. She moved towards Jenny so she could give her the signal.

She didn't want to hurt anyone but was more afraid for the hurt headed towards that young girl. What those young boys could do.

Who their fathers had been.

Chapter Two

Amma and I lucked out. She must know my cycle better than me. My period has never been reliable. I can predict it by my mood, I start to really overthink and I suppose lately I have had too much time to do that anyway.

She'd told me her plan. I'd wear my menstrual cup when I went for my virginity certification. The Senior Queens who had been trained to do the test would be too shy to force the issue. This was more ceremony than anything else. Amma had learned Preston Senior himself would be attending the wedding. It was a big deal to show how he forgave too. Every action he took was out of love for us, his citizens.

Amma was worried for this portion of the plan but once she learned I had gotten my period she was full of joy. For the first time she was happy to hear about my period. She had known that if there was some mistrust, if they pushed at Central Home and Hearth and made me take my cup out, the Senior Queens would be considered dirty. Forced to step to the Red Room at the Central Home and Hearth, despite the fact that most likely they were menopausal. Worker-wives were required to do everything while menstruating. For Queens, they could not be seen. They were impure for these few days each month. And if they weren't menstruating but came into contact with women who were, they became unclean too. And their Knights would be terribly upset to lose extra nights that month with their Queen. It was an effective system to keep the Queens apart and to track their pregnancies.

But we didn't know which Senior Queen would be doing the inspection. Maybe she'd insist to see the cup, to make sure that I was really menstruating. It was her reputation on the line after all. And with Knight's oversight. Or under it.

But I must give thanks to whoever blessed me with the red curse. I woke up that morning with cramps and when I went to the bathroom, saw the color of rust when I wiped. We would be safe. We had the upper hand.

When we arrived back at the motel, Amma helped me get ready for bed. She explained a few things. Jay was looking to get married very quickly. It had looked very bad for Knight when the news broke about Padmini. She had been given the power to punish men. It would be tough for Jay to repair this lie to so many men. How many Knights had been scarred by her over the years? Some went mad afterwards with the shame, killed themselves.

Jay had lied to Knight. Let him know that they had thought they were common law married. They had been exclusive to one another their whole relationship he had lied on his broadcast. Knight had sympathy. And also, people told him what they thought, that Padmini and Jay should be held to a higher punishment. The hardest of labor for both.

But Knight needed Padmini. The Knights relied on her for so much. Sure, the Queens used her products for beauty, she had just released a new tincture that made your pupils dilate, it was the newest trend, even if it was hard to remember things when you took a few drops. Beauty hurts sometimes. The Knights needed her medications as well. They were rationing the pharmaceuticals that remained for the Knights and Queens who really needed them. Their health was a priority, if anything happened to them the whole system would become unstable. There was no telling when other countries would begin trading with us again. If we would open up trade to other regions any time soon. No pharmaceutical company supported us, do no harm if it impacts overall profit with the rest of the world.

And Knight needed Padmini's help cultivating new types of flowers.

"Of course, you self-medicated. Your purpose was taken from you."

Knight wanted to help you with your pain. And life right now was very painful. We were all being asked to make tough choices. Live with our tough decisions. If you needed to take a couple of drops after work, who could blame you. And if you needed a few drops in the morning to make it through the day, well that was ok. Just don't use it during the day, that would be theft after all.

And worker-wives could use a little relief sometimes too. It may even help them during their time with their husbands, if the husband was generous enough to share, you mustn't be rude.

Knight needed drugs to make everyone ok with how things are. To make them need him. Never acknowledging that he needed Padmini. Not Jay.

I can only guess who slipped the news about Padmini and Jay. Leaked it to the paparazzi. It was working out very well for one family at least. Knight had approached Jay personally. They'd had a good working relationship. It would look very badly for Knight to punish the man who helped him rise to power. His first celebrity endorsement. Jay's voice was critical to the Knights' morale. But it was too big a misstep. Jay and Padmini had taken advantage of Knight's generosity. He could have chosen any town to be a Knight's hub. He could have gotten anyone to read a few books on farming and taken over the greenhouses. Couldn't he?

Padmini had approached her, Amma told me, had asked Amma for help. This scandal broke while I was locked in their basement. There was no way to get me out. Amma let Padmini know she would come up with a plan. And prayed.

She woke up in the middle of the night with the solution. She said that she knew if she could have told me, I would have been so happy with it. Raj would marry Padmini, our family would always have access to operations if a problem arose for the Knights. Padmini's title, Queen or not, was up to Knight; what matters is Knight and his citizens would never have to see Padmini in power again. She would have been suitably punished for a Queen. After all, Jay was the Knight. What could Padmini have done? Jay was in charge. Padmini would be the first to wear a black-on-black headscarf. She'd still be setting trends.

As for Jay? He was a dear old friend. He deserved a Queen and Knight would appoint him one. Amma had asked Raj to approach Jay with the proposal. His younger sister, a very good Indian girl. I was old, yes, but I was as innocent as any of the other pre-Queens. Amma had worked her whole life to shelter me, I had only been allowed to study or help with the businesses. They never saw me, did they? And they were able to verify I had never been checked out as a worker-wife. Records showed Jay had paid a monthly fee to make sure I stayed pure. I asked Amma why he had done that and she told me she had begged Padmini to ask him to. She still didn't know. Amma had paid the fee upfront. And now it was paying off.

All that was left was for me to pass my virginity test. Raj had to escort Amma and me. He still wasn't speaking to Amma. Or me. He hasn't let me see Abha since I've been home. I don't even know if she knows that I'm here. That I ever left. What did they tell her? And Amma has denied having sent Tulika to send me her message. I tried two times and the second time she got so upset, told me I hadn't even been home one day and was ruining things. No more questions Swati.

Cindy and Jenny were in formation. They were doing a classic, it should have been easy. Jenny goes in, she acts dumb, asks for food, she begs, she's hungry. Cindy takes out the leader. Jenny picks her choice. Cindy kills. Jenny kills. Cindy always watching Jenny. Following Jenny's lead. She's the one in the fight.

Cindy hadn't wanted to kill anyone. Especially kids. She cried over it. How many lives have been lost? How many mothers have lost their babies? How many mothers were forced to have babies? Just to be killed.

She signaled to Jenny to pull back.

Cindy couldn't kill anyone else. Not today. Especially not kids. They'd have to come back and help that girl somehow. Or leave them alone. She didn't want to kill kids.

She'd had to do it before. Too many times. Twice she'd picked kids up, wanted to adopt them, only to wake to them trying to kill her daughter. Jenny hadn't wanted them to join. Jenny had wanted to kill them. Twice Cindy had picked kids up and they'd been pawns for the men of the borderlands. Jenny and Cindy would make fine rape slaves. Like this poor girl had been taken as.

Both those times Jenny and Cindy had to kill everyone. There was no letting those kids escape back to their clans. Now Cindy would have to wait. See what the situation was. Were they working for someone else? Were men in charge here? Or these boys?

She knew what would happen if she sent Jenny in. Whoever was in charge, the boys would see a rape slave, a way to eat, a way to trade. What had she been thinking? She so desperately wanted to save this young girl she was risking her own daughter's future.

Cindy couldn't live with herself whether she murdered or walked away. Either way all she saw was suffering and she wasn't doing anything about it.

Jenny wanted to kill. Cindy saw it in her eyes. When Jenny looked into her momma's eyes she saw Cindy's pain.

She has to work hard to but somehow she trusts that her momma has another way.

Chapter Three

It'd only been a few hours since I'd left the closet and already so much had changed. It feels so dumb to even write that down. Of course they have. Things have changed.

I'm a pre-Queen. After years of hiding, of being hidden by everyone, I am going to be put on display. Inspected.

Whenever I used to feel like this, out of control, like I couldn't handle the changes, I'd just put on my sneakers and fucking run. I couldn't even run a mile at first. And then all of the sudden, one day I could.

I got hurt too. One time I was three miles away from town and I pulled my hamstring, had to hobble back. A mile of my attempt to get home and a pick-up stopped. I was terrified. This is how I'd die. Or worse, get locked in a room somewhere as a sex slave. I was more afraid of the second, it's hard to believe that today.

It was Adam in the truck. It made me a little less nervous, but I was still scared. He intimidated me. Something about him. But he convinced me. And he didn't try anything. Offered to take me to Padmini's and I asked him to take me back to the motel. I was met with silence so I felt I had to explain, "That way my mother won't know."

"I hate to break it to you Swati, I know you love to run, but if you can't put weight on your leg, your mom is going to find out."

This time I met him with silence. Adam didn't know I didn't want Amma to see that I had been alone with a boy. I had to get back to the motel before she did.

Nothing happened. I learned a little about him. He'd met Jay when he was in the Air Force. They became friends online. When he got out, Jay invited him to move here. Helped set him up. Jay needed help on the farm. Boring stuff. Chores. Security. Adam didn't have any family who cared about him. That's why he was working so hard, he wanted to make a home for himself here.

I smiled and asked questions. Wanting to learn more but not really caring. Nothing would come from this. And what about Jay. Was I waiting for him? I wasn't, but how could I do that to him? I felt something but didn't know how Adam felt.

Adam dropped me off at the motel, watched me unlock the door to my room. We waved and then he drove away. Nobody saw. I was terrified for weeks that Raj had seen at the motel and would use it as blackmail somehow. But nothing happened. Amma and Papa didn't even take me to the doctor for my hamstring. They gave me some old muscle relaxers and handed me a pair of ancient and used crutches. It didn't take as long to heal as I had feared. Still, those weeks I couldn't run away from The Chai House and my family were the hardest. Harder than the closet. I want Amma to know that. I want her to know that I know that.

But she would never really believe me, know what I'm capable of. She doesn't think that highly of me. She has made that crystal clear to me. When she was my age, she ran two successful businesses, had two (what she described to strangers as perfect) children, all with no help, she claimed. She was happily married and friends with everyone in our town. At my age I have nothing. Not one single friend. And I can't even run away from that.

It's Amma's world and I'm just living in it.

I do luck out sometimes though. A lot of the time. Where would I be without her? Amma doesn't think highly of me because I cannot do what she does. She's so independent. I'm really dependent. Everything I do, I have to ask for help, ask for permission.

Raj dropped Amma and me off at the main doors of the Central Home and Hearth. It was important that we didn't walk from the parking lot, we'd be safest under the guard of the Knights protecting the building and the women inside. The world's most modern and intimidating valet system.

Raj met us at the Knights' valet and then escorted us to the registration desk. The Knights guarding the desk pointed him to the Knights' waiting area. A Senior Queen was called to come escort us. The woman at the registration desk had a similar head covering to Amma's. A lighter grey but with crosses. The woman who arrived had a different head covering, it had white with black crosses on it. I'd never seen one before. Neither Amma or I have ever needed to come here. Or I should say, I've never come here. Had Amma been here before? She said yes to the tour when the Senior Queen asked. This would make our appointment much longer than necessary, I just wanted it to be over. I was sweating even though it was freezing in the building.

The Senior Queen introduced herself to us as Marian. No need for titles. As long as we were here, we should make the time after the certification to schedule an appointment to attend their orientation. Marian suggested this politely, as though going through my virginity certification exam was a happy day for me, "If we get a date after the certification, it'll only be a few months before you're in here with your little one!" She smiled at us non-stop.

We started the tour. It was shorter than I thought it would be. There wasn't much we could see, that we were allowed to see, mainly the Knights waiting area and cafeteria. They did have a swimming pool but it was only for Queen usage. Amma gave me a sharp look, it was stupid of me to ask, like they'd let anyone who wasn't a fellow Queen see their swimsuits? I wonder if they swim in the nude or if they had to remain modest. I never understood that about Knight's God. The way they treat us you'd think they'd want us walking around naked all the time.

It was the same thing with The Red Room. Marian told us that I'd spend days and nights there, but they wouldn't allow me to visit it until I was a Queen. Privacy reasons. They don't want folks to know when a Queen is on her period. It's embarrassing. Not only is she unclean, but she has also failed her Knight. It's a hard standard to live up to but they want a Queen to give birth once per calendar year. Everyone knows that the citizen population rates were plummeting. Lots of deaths from things no one would have died from years ago.

Jay really pushed holistic treatment during the hog flu epidemic. Counseled Knight not to pursue the vaccine, insisted we'd build immunity and they could push more apothecary products if people were in pain or needed soothing. People liked using those products a lot more than anything they could get at the medical clinics. And then they didn't have to deal with a doctor. Someone telling them what to do. Telling them how to live. That they weren't as smart as they thought. That they didn't know as much about illness as someone who had studied the science of medicine for a decade, if not more.

The Queens portion of the building was nicer than anywhere I've been to in at least ten years. Once we left the first floor, we didn't encounter a single Knight. Not one man for Amma to shield me from. Not one man to protect us from anyone or anything. It was eerie. I realized the only other time I've been like this is when I was in the closet. And even then I knew I was surrounded by Knights. When Amma would hide me away in The Chai House it was the same thing, I was there but knew there were Knights coming and going. Here, no Knights anywhere. I don't hear their boots, the jingle of their metal identification tags.

We got to a huge, beautiful, waiting room with floor to ceiling windows letting the sunshine in. Marian explained this was their party room, The Sunshine Room, named that way because they also used it to sun in. We didn't often get the vitamin D we need being cooped up, helping out our Knights so much. And we couldn't be outside sunbathing if the opportunity arose, too tempting for the Knights to see a beautiful Queen. "It's just as much our responsibility to protect the Knights as it was theirs to protect us," Marian lectured, still smiling. I'd heard this ages ago. I wouldn't be in trouble if I hadn't tempted Mark. Why did I stay after to help him? I stayed after all the other students had left. He was tempted by how special I was. How precious.

If I passed my test, got a date, and became a Queen, they'd all greet me in this room, Marian continued. It's where they hold baby showers for one another, anniversary parties, and other events like their monthly Knights pamphlets discussion. A Senior Queen who could read, would recite the pamphlet for the younger Queens who may not be able to read. Amma smiled politely throughout Marian's speech and I knew better than to ask any questions. I can't ruin it for everyone. If I spoke, I would.

We waited in the party room until another Senior Queen arrived. Her headscarf was white with red crosses on it. This I had seen before. Sheriff Paulson had brought Queens by The Chai House before wearing these. Always a group, visiting town for an event or training. Sheriff knew our food was exotic and also safe to eat. Nothing grown in a lab. No risk of anyone getting sick.

As the woman in red crosses greeted us with a thin smile, Marian introduced us to her good friend Jillian. Jillian would be helping me with my certification process today, we could follow her, and Marian would be waiting here for us when we were done. Amma and I walked behind Jillian, down several hallways until we were ushered into what looked to be an exceptionally large master bedroom. Jillian gestured for me to take a seat on the bed and asked Amma to take a seat with her, on the other side of the desk in the room. I sat on the bed and watched as tears began to run down Jillian's face. Amma grasped her hands. How did they know one another?

"We don't have long," Jillian said, "Let's get through the list."

And Amma and Jillian talked while Jillian filled out the forms. Jillian and Amma had met decades ago when Lakshmi Auntie had left Padmini's father. I had thought Amma had been saying women's center and only now did I hear Jillian say the words women's shelter. My heart broke for Lakshmi Auntie. I know the judgement she must have faced, leaving her husband and having all the Aunties and Uncles know.

Lakshmi Auntie had to find support outside of the Indian community, no one wanted to talk to someone living in a women's shelter. I was amazed Amma had continued to help her. "Kya log kahenge?" She cared too much about what others thought. And now I know she hadn't been afraid or worried about being known as bad company after all. She didn't care about her own reputation because she cared so much about Lakshmi Auntie.

Lakshmi Auntie's therapist at the shelter, at the time of her divorce, had suggested joining a support group and unlike the poor woman who had been matched with me in Weight Warriors, she had been matched with Jillian at the shelter. At the center. I didn't learn too much about Jillian's story, just enough to learn that her (now dead) husband had also been a piece of shit. She seethed to Amma her disgust about herself. Reinforcing and supporting these men imprisoning women. But what choice did she have? If it wasn't her, someone more terrible could be in this place. She let us know there was no exam for me today, I wouldn't have to suffer that indignity. She'd given the younger pre-Queens exams of course. They had to say they were completed. She knew us. Knew we could be trusted. But my being on my period today was just extra luck, extra insurance. She could place that on the forms without ever incriminating herself for a reason not to give me the exam. She had a concrete reason why she hadn't.

"They all know the hymen being intact doesn't mean shit, but they are still all obsessed with it. They want to fuck every worker-wife on the town payroll but want their Queen to be pure," Jillian ranted quietly. She had let us know there were no cameras in this room due to the purpose of the suite but that it was best to be careful. I stayed silent anyways. I didn't want to risk losing it all. All of us being sent to labor camps if it got found out that I was a mother. If Tulika was found.

Amma and Jillian were able to reminisce a little longer. Neither had heard from Lakshmi Auntie since the year Knight was elected. Things were happening where she lived too. A global collapse it seemed.

Jillian was sorry to have heard about Padmini, she had known her when she was younger. When she was being bullied at school, teased as Pimply Padmini. I wonder if Padmini still sees herself that way? How she is frozen in Jillian's mind. Jillian did not like or respect Padmini much though, she thought it was such a kindness Amma was showing her, "To allow a woman who was not a virgin to be your only son's Queen. I just don't know if I could do it. Raj is going to face a lot of uphill battles with the Knights all knowing Padmini has been used, used by Jay."

"She'd die." I couldn't stay silent a minute longer.

"Who dear?" Jillian asked.

"Padmini. If Amma didn't help her, no one else would."

"Yes, exactly. No other woman who isn't a virgin can't be a Queen."

Amma gave me a look and I stopped before I said what I wanted to say, 'But you know I'm not a virgin."

So instead "I apologize," came out of my mouth. I know how to zip my own lips.

I didn't understand and it didn't matter. Jillian had just been trying to survive like us, she knew how pointless their virginity tests were, but still she insisted on their system. And ran it. I did understand why, I just didn't like it. *She* had done it the right way. Lost her virginity to her abusive husband on her wedding night and then stayed with him for decades until he died. She'd earned her spot at the top. What had Padmini ever done? Would I think any different if I was Jillian?

Amma being Amma simply smoothed things over for us. Let Jillian know that she was right. Raj did deserve a virgin but Padmini would be marrying a man who had a daughter with a Muslim. They each had a bit of a punishment to atone for, didn't they? And Jillian agreed and gushed again at how kind Amma was. Not only was she marrying her son off to a slut, but she was also a grandmother to a Muslim. We were all lucky Amma was here to help us remember our way, Jillian had said. But all I could think about is how hurt Abha will be once Raj and Padmini have their first child. Amma will love her less than she does today. Amma loves a child less for no reason other than the fact that her mother was born to Muslim parents instead of Hindu ones. My Amma will never understand love. She only understands duty. She only understands rules.

Soon enough our time together came to an end. We followed Jillian down the hallways back to the party room where she gave Marian a nod and waved goodbye to us, said she'd see us soon. Would she? Would she be at the wedding? Marian clapped her hands in delight, "Let's get you a date!"

We followed Marian back to the main floor. She asked if I was excited and I smiled at her shyly. I know how to act. She escorted us to a large conference room and let us know which seats were ours. She said that she knew we could read so we were welcome to page through the folder in front of Amma, it contained information about our wedding ceremony. Nothing that Amma didn't already know, hadn't already negotiated with Jay who had moved it up the command chain directly to Knight himself. The folder contained no wedding details which normally Amma would have been excited about, which vendors to choose for catering, who to get flowers from, who to invite. None of that mattered. The folder was basically Knights we could select to officiate our wedding. Knights whose Queens would like to help with the bride's makeup.

Knights whose Queens do party planning and would be contacting Jay to schedule my debut in The Sunshine Room. Meet my new peers.

This wasn't my wedding. It would have been this way no matter the year, I began to realize. This wedding was Amma's and she'd be getting the catering and the floral contracts. And of course, the venue would be Gallows Park. Lavender sodas AND chai for all - this time watch this woman's mouth get sewn shut for as long as we both shall live folks.

Raj and Jay eventually joined us. I kept my eyes down, hidden behind my pink pre-Queen headscarf. Marian was able to make small talk with the men, bring them drinks and snacks. Then bringing us smaller portions of the same. We ate together but not, the men eating, drinking and talking boisterously; I saw spit fly from Jay's mouth as he spoke. The women did all the same but silently. As Marian stood and cleared the plates I wondered if she missed having worker-wives in here. Or did she look forward to actually doing something? I suppose they couldn't risk the worker-wives learning how well the Queens truly live. Especially Senior Queens in retirement. Would worker-wives be jealous that they were allowed to come here and chit chat with armed Knights? I don't think so. They wouldn't want anything to do with them but I could tell Marian loved her status. Being in charge.

Sad for her that she was only in charge of Amma and I.

When Marian came back she was escorting who we had been waiting for, Preston Knight, Junior. We all stood up. Raj had already been warned and also briefed us, his father called him PJ, even in his public speeches. Preston Jr. hated it, and it was doubtful that I'd need to address him but if I did, it was imperative that I called him Preston, not PJ, not Junior, not The Second. Even if that was his celebrity name. Jay had told Raj that PJ hated having to navigate the course his father had set. Live up to his expectations. So similar to me and Amma. Of course, I wasn't insisting everyone call me The Duke. He wanted to be sure to stand out in his father's court of sycophants.

PJ went around the table shaking the men's hands and then came to Amma and touched her feet. She fought him, insisted he stand in the only way she could without touching him or speaking, just shaking her head no. When he stood he told Amma his father had told him to do that, said Preston Senior had told him this town would not have survived this year without Amma and Raj helping out so much. That was when I learned the whole time I had been hiding, studying in my room and cleaning dishes in the back of The Chai House, Raj and Amma had been working to be just as complicit as Jillian had been. They had worked hard, done it the right way. Amma who believed in bad luck never believed in good luck that same way.

When PJ came to me, he put his hand to my chin to try and force our eyes to meet. I fluttered my eyes up briefly, he was smiling but there was no kindness or light in his eyes to match.

"I couldn't wait to meet you Swati. Such a romantic story, watch out or this Knight may try to buy Jay's land before your date!" PJ joked and at first only Jay chuckled but then Raj joined in. Marian hid her smile behind her hand as a Senior Queen should. Amma and I continued to look down. *'Don't ruin this'*, I thought to myself, trying not to shake while Preston Jr. was holding my face. He released it and then sat down at the head of the table, gesturing for all of us to sit. He looked at Jay and asked, "So when's the date?"

Jay looked at him and said, "Saturday."

My heart dropped to my stomach. That was only four days away.

PJ turned to Raj, "Are there any objections to this date?"

Raj smiled and said, "Saturday it is."

"Well then, let's sign," PJ said, gesturing Marian to his side, a rude customer to his waitress. He asked her to go retrieve the papers. She returned with them along with a cart with more food and bubbling drinks. The Knights signed while Amma, Marian, and I worked to make a celebratory spread. What I'd be doing at The Chai House anyway. This time instead of the Knights eating first, PJ insisted that we join them, that Amma take the first bite.

We women joined them, only to smile politely. We were all old enough to remember lively debates with men, but we all knew much better now. We would speak when invited to. And unfortunately, PJ invited me to.

"I'd love to hear the story of how you and Jay first met, Swati," he requested.

I looked down at my feet, assuming Amma would answer for me. She didn't.

"I met Jay years ago." I mumbled down to my feet. How could I tell this story without mentioning Padmini?

"It would probably be best if I told that story Swati," Jay answered for me, already stepping into his new role as my Knight, "Swati used to visit us all the time, I met her through, well, you know who, and she always caught my eye. There are only two exotic women in our town, and I wanted to keep them for myself. I never needed to check Swati out before, luckily. But I kept her safe, working in Raj's business, and now we will be together, our houses joined, strengthening the Knight family's Union."

"And it really worked out to your advantage, didn't it?" PJ wondered aloud.

"I will be indebted to him. Amma and I thank you and Jay." I spoke firmly. PJ had been questioning Jay and I made it about me. Everyone turned to me, the look in Raj's eyes let me know not to mess this up, don't be a nasty girl, don't be me, "If Jay hadn't arranged for me to be one of his worker-wives, I wouldn't have had this opportunity. He kept me off the worker-wives list for others who may have needed my help. I thank Raj and Amma too. They made sure I had everything I needed at home so that I wouldn't have to leave, and I didn't know the burdens placed on any of them. Without them, I would not have this opportunity today."

"Well, that is a swell attitude Swati," Marian was pleased with my answer, happy to know I was aware that my existence is a burden, "You are going to make a fine Queen for Jay."

PJ seemed displeased with my answer in his eyes but his lips held a smile, "Gratitude for our lots in life makes our lives enjoyable Swati. I am glad you know this and Jay is lucky to be matched with someone who understands this well. Let's drink to Deepali Auntie for doing such a good job with her family."

It was a long ride home from Central Home and Hearth. Raj still wasn't really speaking to me but he exploded at Amma during the drive. I had never lived anywhere but at home and now she was sending me to live with Jay. Raj was insisting that Jay had a sick fetish and was trading one Indian woman for another. He screamed that once I started getting older there'd be nothing stopping him from putting Abha on his list of worker-wives, lining her up for when I retired. And he was right. Jay had a fetish for Indian women. Or exotic women.

But Amma didn't budge. She had moved across the world from the only home she had ever known. And I was her daughter. This was the right move to make. Lives would be saved. Padmini's life would be saved, how could she watch Padmini be punished? Sent away. Killed. She had promised Lakshmi Auntie she would always take care of her daughter. And while Jay would own the apothecary, he would need Raj's help gaining Padmini's expertise. He had met PJ! Preston Knight would be attending our wedding (yes, she said our, not Swati's) because his son, the Duke, was officiating. What an honor for our family. We had expected it would be Sheriff Paulson and this wedding was going to show our new status. We were now connected to the first family. The first family is now tied to us thanks to all our businesses, the plans Amma had laid. They needed us. Abha had time, we would gain more power, with Amma's help, Abha would be able to select any family she wanted to marry into, if we were smart, kept our guard up, we may be related to the first family one day. We could be royalty.

I sat in silence as they argued with one another. Whether they didn't notice or didn't care, it didn't matter to me. Either way, I know they just wished I was gone.

Cindy and Jenny stayed nearby. Cindy wanted to see what was happening in this town. This is exactly why she preferred they just keep wandering. Moving around, looping through the landscape, checking the bird feeders every week or so. She always ended up trying to help. Jenny was young but lectured her about it every time. Her momma's kindness was going to get them killed. Jenny didn't understand why. No need to be kind. Just be smart.

Cindy hadn't held out much hope as they set up to watch the boys. Find out who they had captured the pregnant girl for. She was still tied up to the swing set but the boys had left. They hadn't tried anything with her. In fact, she watched as they threw food at her. Cindy wasn't sure what it was but the girl couldn't pick it up. It was at her feet and her arms were tied behind her back. They watched as the girl tried to wriggle around after the boys had left. She couldn't get the food to her mouth. They watched as she cried herself to sleep.

Cindy stayed up while Jenny slept. She got sleep when she could but knew she wouldn't feel safe sleeping here. They'd have to move further out during the day and Jenny could keep watch while Cindy made another attempt to get some rest.

Towards dawn Cindy saw movement, someone in a Knight's cloak, the hood was pulled up over their head. They approached the sleeping girl. It was too late; Cindy was too far away to try to kill him.

The girl woke up, Cindy watched as her eyes went wide. The hood fell off the Knight's face. The Knight hushed the girl with a finger and mimed tying a bow and snipping it with scissors with their hands. Cindy saw their lips move.

Cindy saw it was a woman wearing that Knight's cloak.

Chapter Four

Amma had an early morning surprise waiting for me the next day. I walked into the kitchen to help with breakfast and Padmini was peeling carrots for halwa. As soon as I saw her I started sobbing. Amma came to me and hugged me for the first time since I'd been home.

"See beti, our bodies know. We aren't blood but we are family. We need to look out for one another. They look out for each other but not us. So, we look out for each other," Amma said as she pulled Padmini out of her chair to force her into a three way hug.

I pulled out of the hug and couldn't stop crying, snot running everywhere. Padmini made her way back to the table to peel carrots and Amma went back to setting up to make chai.

I gasped as I tried to stop crying, moving to the sink to splash cold water on my face and wash my hands. Both helped, brought me back to the present. If anyone should be sobbing, acting like a child, it should be Padmini. She had done nothing wrong. Everything she had built was taken from her. Being handed to me. To the Saxena family.

I sat next to her, making the effort to help peel carrots and she continued to ignore me. What could I say? She never told Amma about me and Jay. She had found out by walking in on us one day. I had disrespected her so much; I had allowed her man to love on me while she was working to feed and clothe him. How could she possibly handle the fact that all she had worked on was being given to me? She couldn't even leave our property, so many Knights hated her, she had sewn shut the lips of their sons, brothers, and fathers. And how many worker-wives thought she should be doing the hardest of labor in the canteens? But instead, she gets to remain a Queen, simply by her status of being the Queen of Knight's Operations. They didn't care about what would happen if they didn't get their flower that allows them to live their bleak lives. Because they didn't know that Padmini was behind cultivating it, they didn't have to worry about what would happen if they couldn't get their flower anymore.

Amma took care of the silence. She didn't want to waste any more time. There were only a few days to plan. She talked at us. We had a lot to get done and had to do all the cooking ourselves, she had already had Raj tell Jay no worker-wives, we've never needed them before and we didn't need them today. Everything could be buffet style. Worker-wives would help serve on my big day but there was no way Amma would let them in her kitchen to curse our cooking. Curse our union. She recited the menu to us, we'd have to keep it simple, Jay had agreed to an all-veg meal at Gallows Park, more for Knight's citizens (Jay's followers) to copy, to buy. Chana masala, veg biryani, raita, and roti for guests. Popcorn, lavender soda, and chai for all who attend. It was unlikely there'd be a cake, but maybe Knight would arrange for it, he was bringing photographers, this was a big opportunity for us all.

"Are you going to wear white?" Padmini asked, looking down at her hands as she worked the carrots through the grater.

I stayed silent; I didn't know what I'd wear but I knew what she was asking.

"Unfortunately, yes beti," Amma tsked her tongue in her reply.

"It's bad luck for you," Padmini spoke to me for the first time since I'd gotten free from her closet, since I'd signed an engagement contract to her man at her own dinner table.

I still didn't know what to say, what she was getting at, what it would mean for Abha if Padmini used her knowledge about my past against me.

"My mother was so upset when I lied and said Jay and I had eloped," Padmini continued, not stopping her work with the carrots, "She asked what I wore and I told her how I wore a white dress I got from St. Paulies. She was upset that I wore a used dress to my wedding and the bad luck that would bring but she was most upset that I wore white. '*There'll be no color for the rest of your marriage,'* is what she had told me. Insisted we go to India, I could wear whatever color I wanted, do it right."

Now even Amma was silent. What could any of us say? Padmini hadn't been able to speak to her mother in years. We had no idea how she was doing. If she was still in India. If she was still alive.

Finally Amma spoke, "Arrey beti, no use to dwell on the past. Now you have a good match, my first son." Amma tickled Padmini in the ribs, forcing a non-consensual laugh. But it was enough to break the ice. Padmini seemed to loosen up.

Amma and Padmini continued to discuss plans. There was a lot to do in two days. Padmini let us know that Jay's worker-wives would be able to take care of the sodas and popcorn for all who viewed the wedding. Raj would get Knights to deliver all of the food. My wedding was going to be a large picnic. That I wouldn't get to enjoy. Jay and I would be on display on stage. Everyone would want to watch us while they ate their meals. How did Jay treat me after the ceremony? Would we share the same cup even after the ceremony or drink chai from our own cups while on display? Would I speak to him while everyone was watching or be demure? And everyone would want to come on stage to have their photos taken with us. Our wedding was being officiated by PJ and his father would be in attendance. Everyone who attends will be able to say they attended a wedding with not one Knight, but two. And their Queens. What would they be wearing? I had to make it stop.

"Enough about me," I interjected, "Padmini, what do you wish for your ceremony with Raj?"

Amma and Padmini just looked at one another.

"Beti, Raj and Padmini are Knight and Queen now," Amma looked in my eyes as she spoke slowly.

"What do you mean?"

"Yesterday, Raj signed for you and Jay signed for Padmini. It won't be good for Padmini and Raj to show off their family now. And we needed to keep her safe. It is best not to draw attention to her right now."

"I don't understand," I stuttered, how could they be married without a celebration? No acknowledgement?

"Swati, you have to try to understand. Both Raj and Padmini have marks against them, it's best not to bring attention to the special treatment and deals they are getting. We are lucky she is even here today, can help with your big wedding day."

"Why does Jay need anyone at all?" I was starting to raise my voice.

"Because I humiliated him Swati," Padmini said to me when she saw I was rising out of my seat.

"How did you humiliate him? I don't understand what is happening. Why couldn't you marry either of them?"

Padmini ran her hands through her hair, getting bits of carrots everywhere, her frustration with me coming out, "There's nothing to understand! We are doing everything we can to survive! Jay didn't want to marry me before and it was too late after when we had done so much to promote and protect Knight! To help him rise to power and disrespect his platform at the same time? Someone needs to pay the price, and I'd rather have an arranged marriage to Raj than be dead. Maybe one day they'll let me leave The Motel or The Chai House but even then, I'll have to worry about people wanting to slice my neck. I'd rather marry into the family doing the killing than being killed."

"What are you saying?" I sobbed, dropping back into my seat, "Why does there have to be any killing?"

“Wake up you stupid girl!”. Amma slapped me to the floor with the force of her open hand, “How can you be so stupid, why does anyone have to die? Just shut up and be happy you are being married to the most powerful man in town. Your dear sister Padmini is safe in our family now. What do you want you stupid?”

How can she slap me, I laughed to myself, what a joyous occasion this is. And Amma was right, what *did* I want? I’ve never known the answer to that question, no one has ever given me the opportunity to discover what I want. Just expectations of who to be.

When Jenny woke up, Cindy told herself. Jenny was old enough. She's had to make some tough decisions. Had to see a lot. Cindy wanted to know what Jenny would want to do, even if she was young.

What would Jenny want? Cindy didn't know what she'd say, whether she would want to go after the woman and girl, join up or run away? Pretend nothing ever happened?

"Momma, I wanted to kill those boys. And her."

"Oh honey, you weren't sure what was best for her. So, we slowed down. Got more intel."

"Momma. I don't want to be here anymore. I don't want to go find those two."

"That's ok sweetie. Let me get some rest and we'll figure out what to do next." Cindy smiled at her daughter.

They wouldn't be getting any textbooks soon. But it was ok, Cindy thought to herself, I didn't get a parenting textbook and I'm doing ok.

Chapter Five

Tomorrow's the big day. Amma's taken care of all the details. *All I have to do is show up* is what I keep telling myself. I can handle that. I've been handling that. Today's a big day for me though. Amma, Raj, and even Padmini and Abha get to come along to the home inspection. It's a chance for the pre-Queen's family to become familiar with her new home. We have to stick with the routine, nobody knows that I know the house, including a particular closet, well enough already. It would look bad on Raj if word got out that he skipped the inspection or that we rejected Jay's invitation. So, although no one but Amma wants to go, a grand tour and supper with the two families it is.

It doesn't matter that it will be just our family and Jay. He doesn't have a family since Padmini was taken away. It was kind of Knight to let Jay sign for Padmini. Act as her male guardian although he wasn't. Some rules can be broken. It was just the two of them for such a long time. Raising their flowers together. But Jay has been relying on Adam a lot lately, maybe he will be there tonight. For some reason, I'm hoping he will be there tonight.

I'm glad Padmini is coming and I'm also nervous. Does Jay still love her? I've been thinking of the sounds of his orgasms with her, after visiting me, just a week ago. I can't stop thinking of Tulika either. She's got to be a worker-wife at Jay's place. Soon, maybe I'll get to see her. Spend time with her every day if she's been checked out by Jay. But what if what he said was true? What if the reason Raj was worried about Abha was true? What if it came true for Tulie? I haven't had a chance to ask Padmini. I've been too scared. I don't want to burden her more than I already have. She never knew I was pregnant. I'll sound crazy.

So, I wait. I don't have much to pack. Pretty much everything I packed when I was planning to run north. My vacation getaway to the closet. I've been worrying about what my days will look like starting tomorrow. Padmini had so much independence, she ran the whole operation. Amma told me there'd be no need for that, but I'd be expected to take on a few of Padmini's other duties. I would be the new Queen Patron of Punishment. Amma had already negotiated it with Jay and Knight. It made everything seamless. I've never hurt anyone in my life (well, physically) and now I'll be sewing Knights lips shut while crowds munch on popcorn and sip on their lavender tea. I told Amma that I don't even know if I can stand being around someone in pain and she told me I'd be able to. What was the alternative? It was me or them. Who would I choose? Did I want her to talk to Padmini to find a tea that might help me relax before the first few sewing ceremonies? It was OK if I needed something to help me do this work.

Years ago, Padmini offered me friendship, an escape from my family, an escape from this world. All that she offered me, and I chose myself over and over, even after watching her choose herself second over and over. What do I want? For Padmini to be free. For Abha to be free. For every single worker-wife to be free. For every woman to be free. For everyone to be free. But that won't happen in my lifetime. There's nothing I can do today that would stop the Knights from taking what *they* want. There will always be someone who doesn't want us to be free. Who wants to be in charge.

So, I'll be compliant. Help Amma shape rotis. Keep myself clean and have Amma plait my hair. Wear the clothes she lays out for me today. Be a presentable pre-Queen. It's my last day of it. Tomorrow I'll be a Queen.

The wedding is still on but so much has changed. Again, in only a few hours. In just a few days. Amma let me know there'd be a change in plans. Again. But to do everything as planned. I won't have to worry about a thing. Just show up and get married. Everything will be ok.

When we arrived Adam was there, I was so happy to see him. I don't know him, but he seems nice. He has never overstepped. He made it seem like he didn't want anything. I am excited to get to know him. It was no surprise it was only Adam; Jay has no family. I suppose that goes into the shared hurt between him and Padmini. When Jay was just 15, he fought for emancipation from his parents. They had kept trying to make him a Hollywood success story but in doing so, had burned through all of that sweet *10 Items or Less* money. They had really hurt him. Put him in dangerous situations. They both ended up in prison, they were at least both there when Padmini had moved back to town with Jay, which was just another thing to hide from Amma and Papa. They didn't want me hanging out with such bad company.

At dinner Jay explained that Adam was moving in, we had space after all. Jay had hated that his next in charge went home to sleep at a Knights' Boarding House every night, and anyway, we needed the help now that Padmini would be in more of a consulting role. I noticed Amma and Padmini exchange glances but couldn't figure out why. The inspection went fine, although I can't say I know what a bad inspection would look like. Abha had fun, to Amma's horror she played with the chickens. Amma couldn't do anything to stop it though, Jay insisted and even Raj smiled watching her chase them around. Amma made her wash her hands all the way up to her shoulders afterwards.

Jay mentioned he wanted to expand the farm, did Raj and Amma have thoughts on other animals that would help fill *our* family coffers? Raj and Amma politely discussed but both tried to defer the conversation. Neither wanted to be further tied down with Jay and his wild ideas and they knew it was already too late. Cows, goats, or alpacas? No one here knew how to take care of any of them but Jay would make a decision soon. It was important to keep broadening their trade offerings. Our trade offerings.

Dinner was a nice surprise. It kind of felt like old times. Jay had surprised us by having Sal over earlier in the day to make pizzas for us. He had also prepared salads for us and to everyone's delight, we had baked apples for dessert. I started to have a little hope, if Jay got a cow, one day Abha would be eating fresh ice cream with her baked apples. The conversation was light, it felt familial, like everyone else had hope too. When we were done eating Raj took Abha out to the porch swing, she had admired it when we walked up the front steps. Would she have memories of this night? Swinging with her dad out here, looking at the stars? Probably not, she's so young.

Padmini started to clear the dishes and I began to help, and then Jay insisted I sit. While he was telling me that we had something important to discuss, I couldn't stop thinking of Padmini. How strange it must feel to clean up in her own house and then drive home to sleep in Raj's bed. Now, I wonder if Padmini had known. She had to have but it wasn't her place to bring it up when Amma was making her deal. Even if she hadn't, if she had insisted on being sent to hard labor, sent to death, what would Amma have done? I think she'd still accept. "*What do you want?*"

Jay had let us know we needed to renegotiate but under the table. No records could be kept. There would be nothing to sign. Raj could find out, but this wasn't his matter just yet. Only if Jay and Amma couldn't reach a resolution. And only if Amma wanted. If I wanted him to know.

After the certification ceremony Central Home and Hearth had reported to Jay that I was still able to menstruate and would be expected to come in for monthly checkups after our wedding night. They hadn't ever pressured Jay and Padmini about this but it was looking very suspicious that Jay had never produced an heir. Knight was insisting he have a family, the citizens want to see Jay as a happy father, what inspired all of his work on the broadcast and on the farm.

If I wasn't pregnant at the fourth visit, they'd test Jay's sperm count. Amma didn't care, she had expected that I would provide an heir. She must not have worried about why Padmini had never had kids. Amma understood working women, that children hold them back. The fathers never help, the work always lands on the mother.

I hadn't realized that until that moment. I had never asked Padmini if she wanted kids one day. If she was excited to be Abha's stepmom. This was also when I realized Adam was staring at me. I hadn't noticed or thought anything about the fact that Jay didn't dismiss him earlier, ask him to step out of what was a very private conversation.

Jay asked Amma if we understood what he was asking of us and we didn't understand. Neither of us. I thought he was saying we only had a few months to figure out a plan. A new way to escape. Instead, Jay explained how he had had a vasectomy in his early 20s. He always knew he never wanted kids. He didn't want to fuck anyone up how his parents had to him. Except that this would be a second lie for him. Preston Knight Senior wouldn't allow two big mistakes like this. Knight needed a celebrity family to display real family values. In a whisper, Amma asked him what he was saying. Jay said clearly that I would have to sleep with Adam. That I'd be treated as Queen by them both. But only Jay's Queen in public. If Knight had found out that Jay had damaged valuable government property with his vasectomy, he'd have a celebratory execution. Knight wanted population growth. Birth control was not an option for anyone. Queens were a valuable treasure, but they were useless without a Knight. And a Knight was useless without an heir. One per year is what they want us to aim for.

"And what if they found out about me?" I finally spoke.

"They never will. Both Adam and I promise. It would be death for the both of us. For you, you would have been forced into it. You can even say we drugged you," Jay said.

What choice did I have? Amma and I couldn't say no. It was too late. We sat in silence and then Adam spoke, asking, "Is there any way we could make this better? What do you want?"

I've been thinking about this for days, years, and I still don't know. I don't have an answer. But Amma did. Amma knew what she wanted. "We have no choice but to accept, whatever I want. I don't want my daughter to be a whore, no different than a worker-wife. She was promised to be a Queen. After one heir, Adam must move out. And all operations will move under me starting tomorrow. No major decisions can be made or Swati will be placed in the difficult position of having to go to Sheriff Paulson," she finally answered.

I wonder if I'd sew their lips up after Sheriff Paulson got involved. Would that duty be temporarily handed back to Padmini?

Adam looked at me. Jay looked at me. They wanted to know what I wanted. I didn't care that my answer would make Amma upset, that she'd call me stupid, it's all I wanted, all I ever wanted so I finally answered, "Peace. I want to be left alone. To have calm. I want to apologize to Tulika. I want to have friends. I want to be able to run. I want to be able to go where I please. I want to be able to visit my family without asking for permission. I want Abha to be able to read and write."

The look on Amma's face was not one of anger, or a look telling me I was stupid. She translated for me, "Swati wants power."

Jay came and kneeled in front of me. He explained that he hated living under Knight's laws, and that if it were up to him, I would have power. All he could promise me was that he would give me as much power as possible. That we would be equals as much as possible. He left out that if it were up to him, we wouldn't have to marry. But I knew that it was up to him. His celebrity is behind all of this. He helped Knight gain power. Just so he could legalize his flowers. Padmini's flowers. Had it all been worth it?

Padmini came back in the room, apologizing for interrupting. Jay rose to his feet and told her no apology was necessary. It was time to end the night. We'd all be back together at noon tomorrow. Drive home safely and sleep well. Sweet dreams to us all.

I couldn't sleep. I woke up and peeked out my window in time to see Padmini take off on Raj's old bicycle. It'd be safer to walk, if she gets caught by a Knight, there's no excuse she could give. But maybe she's running away. I don't know what cameras work and what cameras don't anymore. I saw her speak to Amma, Amma must have sent her on her way. Given her instructions. I'll wait for her return, I can see that Amma's light is on, she must be waiting for Padmini too.

Cindy and Jenny had decided together. They'd head back towards town. Check the bird feeders and then decide what to do. Cindy needed time to think. How could Deepali help her? She couldn't risk leaving a note.

She decided she couldn't ask Deepali for help anyways. She was already burdening Deepali. Putting her family at risk to help another family out. She fed them however she could. Deepali had wanted Cindy to run up north right away. That way Cindy could help them.

She saw Jenny dancing her happy dance. No movement with her feet. Just hips and arms. It was a way they could celebrate without making a sound.

The bird feeders were hung on green strings today. They'd be eating well if Cindy could sneak into town.

Chapter Six

I fell asleep again. Waking up to you in the same position as I'd find you in the closet, tucked between my bed and the wall and there it came to me. I spent time this morning, as quietly as I could, using scissors and my multi tool, working to remove a side panel toward the floor, I can hide you there. I'll come back for you if I can, and if not, you'll be hidden by my bed. I don't think they'd willingly rent this room out. Amma said I'll always have a room here even if I never use it. I believe her. As long as she's alive, this will be my room.

We came back last night, everyone pretending to be happy about tomorrow for Abha's sake. Lying to her that it was a joyous occasion. Raj tucked Abha in and Amma did the same for me. She told me it was the last time she'd ever be able to. That for every year since I've been in her belly, I've been her beti and I'll always be her little one to protect. I used to always love Amma's bedtime stories, I hadn't had one in so long and she had saved a new one for our last one. I don't know if she was thinking that I'd be sharing it with my kid someday. Jay's kid. Adam's kid. Our kid. Her grandchild. Her heir. Her blood. That is what I had been thinking. She was sad. Solemn. It was one of only a handful of times I hadn't seen her angry about something. Amma was always upset and seeing her this calm was absolutely chilling.

"Once upon a time there was a beautiful girl named Kaira. She lived a happy life at home with her family. When she became of marriageable age, she had a lot of suitors. Her father selected for her a nice, older man from a well-to-do family of merchants, his name was Naveen. Kaira and Naveen grew to live a pleasant life. Kaira never went without. Naveen's family often requested his help with their business, for which he had to travel. And because of this, Kaira was often left home alone. She always kept a clean house, made sure her neighbors had enough to eat, and offered to help them as much as she could but there were still many hours left in the day where she did not have much to do. She came up with an idea to go down to the market every day so that her new family's presence would still be felt and known there. Although she did not shop, she made sure to visit all the market booths to get to know their owners. In this way, she'd be helping her husband, it may mean more buyers when he returned from his travels.

Over time, through her visits to the market, she met a lovely young man, about her age, named Zain. When she'd run into Zain at the market, he would always make her laugh, he'd insist on buying her a mango lassi to stay fresh while they walked, he'd give her inside tips on the merchant's families, and the latest market gossip. Over the months Kaira realized she loved Zain and was just as sure that Zain loved her. They had become the best of friends; Zain knew she was married and did not care. He was not worried about what others may think or that he may be tarnishing Kaira's reputation by taking her out in public. Everyone knew they weren't related after all.

One day Naveen let Kaira know he would be traveling for business. That night she decided she would travel to Zain's home to let him know her true feelings. She could not stand the idea of another night alone in her own bed. She was stupid but also brave. She was sure to bring a machete, that way whoever she ran into, man, animal, or both, she could protect herself. She made it to Zain's home and rapped on his window.

Zain looked out the window and was terrified. He had risen from a nightmare and when he saw Kaira standing outside his window, he had no recognition of who she was. She had been backlit from the moon so all he recognized was a shapely woman with a weapon in her hand. Once Kaira saw the fright in Zain's eye's she hid in his yard, thinking of what she should do next.

As she was deciding whether to go back home and sleep alone or to name herself and ask for permission to enter Zain's home, to declare her love for him, to ask to lie in his bed with him, to give herself to him; she saw two men sneaking towards the home. As these thieves worked to unlock Zain's door, Kaira recognized who they were, her husband Naveen and his younger brother Rishi. She realized how Naveen had made it possible that she never had to go without. How she was able to have everything she could possibly need. When it was safe and she was able to, she ran back home and cried into the pillows upon her bed. There was nothing she could do now and she was scared. All she could do is hope that Naveen had not seen her hiding at Zain's home. She would sleep alone in her bed for the rest of her days as long as it meant no shame came to her family.

A few days later Kaira was arrested along with Naveen, Rishi, and Zain. Zain had gone to the authorities. After Kaira stopped going to the market out of fear, Zain realized that Kaira had been one of the thieves along with her husband and brother-in-law. He believed she had been working with the brothers to take advantage of him. Zain had concluded that she had pursued him so that her husband's family could gain even more riches than they already had. The authorities brought Zain's accusation to the king as they knew that the king had been trying to capture these thieves for years. The brothers had been targeting well-to-do families and selling their stolen goods to markets outside his own kingdom. Kaira tried to explain that she had no idea what happened on her husband's business travels and that she had gone to Zain's that night to declare her love for him; that she was not a thief. And this enraged the king even more. After learning that Zain had led Kaira on, he had him arrested. Zain had known Kaira was married but still openly pursued a friendship with her, knowing that men always wanted one thing from women, it was their nature which is why these laws were in place. To protect women from men. The king knew he needed to remind those he ruled that there was a reason he had laws in place and executed Naveen, Rishi, Zain, and Kaira all together on the same day. There was a reduction in rape and theft for the remainder of his time as a ruler and the king died knowing that his difficult decision to kill his four young citizens had been worth it, it was all for the betterment of his kingdom, so that his citizens would be safer every day and every night."

Amma kissed me on the cheek and told me to have sweet dreams, which I did not. I had a lot of trouble falling asleep. Amma let me know she'd help me get ready today so I am going to say good-bye to you here. I need to shower and want to be sure I hide you properly. There's room for my Gamer Girl there too so you won't be alone. I won't have much time to play games as Jay's Queen.

Part Three

The Beginning of The End

"Momma, what does this say? I can only make out some of the letters," Jenny whined. She was tired, hungry, curious, and impatient.

"You will have to wait darling," Cindy said to her daughter quietly, still unpacking all the food from the box Deepali had left for her outside of The Chai House, next to the dumpster. Her senses were heightened right now, it had been eerily quiet when she had snuck into town to grab the basket. She had picked up that there had been an event at Gallows Park that morning and was worried when she saw Deepali's signal coincided with her pick-up order. She trusted Deepali though. Deepali wasn't one to make mistakes.

Cindy and Jenny were hungry most days and Deepali would never put them at risk, she knew they'd be able to manage on their own without food. Deepali would never risk Jenny losing her momma for food that was meant for the trash. Even if Deepali was confident that Cindy was always sure to make sure Jenny knew how and where to hide and what her priorities were if Cindy didn't come back after two sunsets.

Deepali knew Cindy was a warrior.

Deepali had packed a lot of food for them in that box. There had never been so much. Cindy didn't think that it would even be possible for them to eat it all without it going bad. Cindy didn't know what Deepali had been thinking but she hadn't arranged a pickup for them in nearly a month. Deepali was probably feeling guilty. She always worried about them. Cindy had been really worried about Deepali too. Cindy knew things were bad for Deepali's friends in town. When Deepali could safely get food and medicine to them, she would. And she always did.

But still it had been so eerie. As Cindy snuck her way over to The Chai House, the town had been absolutely still. It was like one of those horror movies you'd watch for fun before all this went down, before we all voted Knight into power. You were afraid just because of how still and silent the movie was. That was your signal that something bad was coming. You were on edge, ready to scream. To grab the arm of whoever was sitting next to you. To keep you safe.

This is how Cindy felt most hours of the day anyway. She got back to Jenny with the box as quickly and quietly as possible. Cindy was always so fucking scared, waiting for the next bad thing to happen to them. Jenny was used to it. She'd be excited to open the box. See what Deepali Auntie had packed them. Cindy was sure Jenny couldn't remember her, but she wanted to make sure Jenny knew there were people who helped. They were hard to find but they existed. And it was up to us to decide if we wanted to be helpers or not. If we wanted to be kind.

Cindy thought about how Deepali had helped them escape. She couldn't help them with a place to stay or protect them with weapons, but she kept them fed. This was how Deepali knew how to help. She made it so that Cindy didn't have to be a worker-wife. So that Jenny wasn't taken from her, indoctrinated into the ignorant Knight cult. "Just until this is over, let me help you," is what Cindy will never forget, "you have to run." Deepali putting her own family at risk for a customer she admired but who she didn't really even know.

Deepali had noticed Cindy's demeanor and picked up that she had been in the army, learned that Cindy had left that life when she wouldn't take one of the private militia's offers and it was decided women could not be in the armed forces. For safety, biological reasons, and whatnot. Deepali had faith that Cindy would be able to take care of herself and her daughter for as long as she could. Deepali had instructed her to stay safe because one day she herself may need Cindy's help to fight Knight. She pulled out of her headspace and asked Jenny for the note, wanting to read Deepali's careful handwriting before Jenny could, suddenly very afraid and not ready to share whatever the content may be with her ten-year-old daughter.

All I can do is hope that you saw my signal and were able to get to town before others found us. Whatever you may think of my actions, it's important that you know it was my only choice. I don't trust anyone in town and none of us could be saved. If I had let anyone know of my plans, they would have tried to stop me. I know you will be disgusted by my actions, but this war has gone on long enough. I came here for a better life for my daughter and instead both my daughter and granddaughter will have less freedom than I ever did. I don't know if I can ever explain my actions to you in a way that you'd understand. You've given everything up for your daughter, and now because of me, you must run. But also because of me, you have the opportunity to run far away. A head start. If you're reading this, Knight is dead. Or soon will be. All of the town's Knights are as well. I had help but you cannot blame anyone but me. I asked for help but lied about my plan. I didn't want anyone to stop me. If I killed only the Knights, the townspeople would have come after our family. If not, we would be killed to set an example by whoever took over after Knight. If I killed everyone but my family, there would have been strife among us. Always a fight over what was right and what was wrong. We would never ever have peace. I thought about how I could get Abha to you but realized she'd never be safe. She'd be put to death too. So it was best the way I did it. Everyone went peacefully. Had a good time even. Enjoyed the wedding, the cake, and my special blend of tea. I hope they did. The only good from all this death is if in our last moments on earth, we were at peace together. I don't want my family to be scared any longer. Take this box and run. As fast and far north as you can. It's on you to save yourself from these men and these militias. The moment I met you I knew you could fight, you'd killed men at war. I don't know if you were forced to kill civilians when you were at war. Maybe you'll understand, maybe you won't. Just know that I did the best that I could for the people of this town, tried to make the best of the situation and realized the best situation was the one where Knight was no longer in power. And I couldn't wait for someone else to take his power away. It could be his son or another warlord. Either way, the result would be the same for us. So run, you need to fight, I could never kill in war, but I could kill in peace to help you overpower these men. Run and fight. Run and live. Run and play with your daughter. Teach her. But for now, it's no longer safe for you here and you won't find help any longer. I hope my actions don't end your lives too. Leave.

Cindy looked over at Jenny, tears in her eyes. Fucking Deepali had killed everyone with her fucking tea. She hadn't waited for Cindy's help. Their plan to gain power and weapons and fight back. Instead Deepali had gone ahead with her plan on her own. She'd floated the idea of a weak, poisonous tea to Cindy, get the Knights sick, make them weak so they wouldn't be able to fight, so there'd be less of them when Cindy had finally organized enough power to try and take the town back. Instead, Deepali had been pushed off the deep end and made her tea blend completely toxic. Soon there'd be a smell coming from Gallows Park that would alert all the folks of the borderlands that the town was available to be claimed. She had to get Jenny out of there before they ran into anyone looking for a fight or looking for food.

"Alright kiddo," Cindy said to Jenny, "I think we have a bit of walking to do tonight. Let's have a few bites here to energize us as we walk."

"It's nighttime Momma," Jenny whined.

"The best time to travel. No one will see us and no one on the roads. You know that girl."

"Ok Momma. But what's in Deepali Auntie's note?"

"Let's play spelling bee instead while we eat darling. That way you won't have to rely on me as much to read Deepali Auntie's notes."

In between spell checking Jenny's vocabulary Cindy plotted their route north. When they were a bit further out, they were able to stop and Cindy unpacked the box, filling their pockets and bags with the snacks Deepali had provided them for their travels. At the very bottom of the box Cindy found two mason jars full of tea leaves, both labeled Do Not Drink. *Cindy thought carefully about whether or not to pack them, worried it may implicate her if they were found running away. She looked over at Jenny playing spelling bee, using a stick to write her vocabulary into the dirt before spelling aloud, that wasn't cheating, it was practice, Cindy always said. Knowing how to spell out loud would be no help to Jenny if anything happened to her. Cindy packed the tea in her satchel, the one Jenny knew never to touch, it's where she kept her gun and Jenny could really hurt herself if she played with it. She thanked Deepali silently for giving her the tea, a more peaceful alternative to the gun for her if she ever needed to use it. Cindy looked at the stars in the sky and prayed to her ancestors to keep her and Jenny safe so she'd never have to use it.*

She looked over to Jenny and saw her drawing constellations in the dirt. Cindy kicked dirt over her daughter's words and drawings and held out her hand.

"It's time to walk. What should we play?"

"I see the North Star Momma!"

"Constellations it is darling."

Acknowledgements

Mom and Dad, thank you will never be enough. You gave up a lot so that I could experience a life that would never have been possible without you. Thank you for all of the sacrifices you made so that I could have a better future.

I couldn't have written this book without my best friend ACJ. You inspire me every day and you have taught me how to hold myself accountable without beating myself up. I wrote the first version of this story in 2017 when you gifted me a vacation and I was able to wake up and write while watching the sun rise over the ocean. I'd never done that before. This was entirely possible because of you.

BRG there is absolutely no way I could have completed this without your support. All I've ever wanted was to be loved by you and you've given me that and so much more. I have no idea how I got so damn lucky. Your belief in me makes me believe in me. I know you know I love you, more than words, like turtles all the way down. You're the one and I'm so glad you know it. I'm really ding dang lucky.

And when I talk about lucky, how is it possible that I found such a supportive Didihood? I had to step away from our WhatsApp and when I returned and announced I had completed this story, your reaction was everything. You've taught me so much this year. I can't wait for our trip to the motherland.

SZ and MM, I am glad you know what a synopsis is now. Looking forward to seeing you in our retirement villa Golden Girls style. Please don't make me go to any reunions. And seriously, thank you. Your pride in me makes my heart swell. I'm really proud of you too.

LSC I'm so grateful for your friendship. You always let me be stupid around you and for that I say, haha you love me! And you know I love you back, right? Right.

NG and SJ. Thank you for inviting me into your families. I feel so loved by you.

AM. I am so grateful to you. I have learned so much from you this year. The number of times since June I have told myself, "don't be ashamed, are they ashamed?" when I've challenged myself to speak up. You have helped me become someone who helps *others* speak out. Your friendship and mentorship has changed my life. Thank you for editing this book and thank you for fighting for justice with me.

Printed in Great Britain
by Amazon

82252554R00072